D0485793

FIRE TRAP!

Frank leaped out into the sky and began counting. One thousand one . . . one thousand two . . . one thousand three . . . one thousand four . . .

Frank heard a rattle of fabric, and the chute grabbed him. He threw his head back to check the rigging. Everything looked good. Then he glanced down at the burning forest—things didn't look so good down there. He was drifting too close to the fire. Frank pulled on the toggle in his left hand, letting a jet of air escape from an opening in back of the chute.

The chute swerved away from the fire as the ground came up fast. Frank clamped his feet together and rolled forward as he hit. But his chute caught the wind and began to drag him toward the fire. Frank clawed at his harness release, but he couldn't get a grip on it.

The chute hit the fire and burst into flames. . . .

Books in THE HARDY BOYS CASEFILES™ Series

Available from ARCHWAY Paperbacks

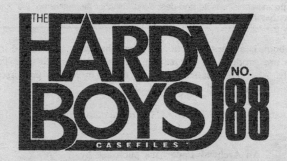

THE HARDY BOYS CASEFILES NO. 88

INFERNO OF FEAR

FRANKLIN W. DIXON

AN ARCHWAY PAPERBACK
Published by POCKET BOOKS
New York London Toronto Sydney Tokyo Singapore

The sale of this book without its cover is unauthorized. If you purchased this book without a cover, you should be aware that it was reported to the publisher as "unsold and destroyed." Neither the author nor the publisher has received payment for the sale of this "stripped book."

This book is a work of fiction. Names, characters, places and incidents are products of the author's imagination or are used fictitiously. Any resemblance to actual events or locales or persons, living or dead, is entirely coincidental.

AN ARCHWAY PAPERBACK *Original*

An Archway Paperback published by
POCKET BOOKS, a division of Simon & Schuster Inc.
1230 Avenue of the Americas, New York, NY 10020

Copyright © 1994 by Simon & Schuster Inc.
Produced by Mega-Books of New York, Inc.

All rights reserved, including the right to reproduce this book or portions thereof in any form whatsoever. For information address Pocket Books, 1230 Avenue of the Americas, New York, NY 10020

ISBN: 0-671-79472-8

First Archway Paperback printing June 1994

10 9 8 7 6 5 4 3 2 1

THE HARDY BOYS, AN ARCHWAY PAPERBACK and colophon are registered trademarks of Simon & Schuster Inc.

THE HARDY BOYS CASEFILES is a trademark of Simon & Schuster Inc.

Cover art by Brian Kotzky

Printed in the U.S.A.

IL 6+

Chapter

1

JOE HARDY SWATTED at a swarm of buzzing insects. "Forget grizzlies!" he muttered. "The most dangerous animals in Alaska are mosquitoes."

"Okay," said Frank Hardy, following his younger brother up the narrow game trail to a rock ledge. "In that case you fight the grizzlies and I'll fight the mosquitoes. But slow down. The rest of the group must be a quarter mile behind us."

Joe paused, impatiently wiping away mosquitoes and sweat from his forehead. It had been eighteen-year-old Frank's idea to spend a week of summer vacation hiking in the Alaskan wilderness. Frank had sent off for a brochure from Bull Moose Treks, an adventure outfit based near Alaska's Denali National Park. Frank had even

1

convinced their father, the famous detective Fenton Hardy, to help pay for the plane tickets to Anchorage and the train fare to Denali Park.

Now that they were here, though, it was seventeen-year-old Joe who couldn't wait to reach the top of the first mountain. Paul Garcia, the owner of Bull Moose Treks and their guide for the week, had promised they'd have a perfect view of Mount McKinley, the highest point in North America, from there.

"Here come the others," Frank said, brushing his brown hair off his forehead. "I hear them talking."

Looking back the way they had come, Frank could just make out Paul Garcia, a tall, dark-haired young man in his twenties, pushing through the underbrush. Three other young trekkers, dressed in baggy shorts, backpacks, and hiking boots, trailed behind him. Except for a brief lunch stop two hours earlier, the group had been climbing steadily uphill since seven that morning. It was now past two in the afternoon, and the pace had definitely slowed.

"It sure smells great up here," Frank said as the others drew near.

"You mean that minty aroma? That's labrador tea," Paul called up to him. "It's a shrub used by native Alaskans to cure indigestion."

"You guys shouldn't have gone ahead," added Barbara Smullen as the group reached the ledge on which Frank and Joe stood. A tall, athletic eighteen-year-old from Akron, Ohio, Barbara was on her third Bull Moose wilderness hike in three years. She hooked a strand of blond hair behind her ear. "You missed something really awesome. We saw a big old grizzly!"

"Where was it?" Joe asked, munching on some berries he'd picked along the trail.

"Grazing in the brambles, back by that old prospector's shack," Paul said with a twinkle in his brown eyes. "It looks like you and the grizz stopped at the same place."

"It was unbelievable," Alex Loggins, a thin seventeen-year-old from Flint, Michigan, chimed in. "The bear was swallowing whole bushes."

Joe glanced down the trail. "What kept the bear from swallowing *you?*"

Paul shrugged as if it was no big deal. "The wind was blowing toward us, so the bear didn't know we were there," he said. "If it had caught our scent, it would've stood up on its hind legs to get a look at us. Then it probably would have hightailed it over the next ridge."

"What if one comes after you?" Frank asked.

"The best thing to do is stand your ground, wave your arms around, and shout," Paul answered. "If that doesn't work, fall down and play dead."

"What's the third best thing to do?" asked Alex.

Paul grinned. "There isn't one. You can't outrun a grizzly, and you sure can't outfight him. All you can do is stay out of his way. That's why I always tell my hikers to use their heads—in the wilderness, your smarts are what keep you alive."

"How smart do you have to be to survive out here?" said Sam Norris, a rangy twenty-year-old from Denver. Sam's hair was cut short on top but left long in the back so it flowed over his collar. "The mountains must be full of food and places to find shelter."

Frank glanced at Joe, who rolled his eyes.

"Right—and if you tried to live out here by yourself, you'd probably starve to death in three weeks flat," Paul said. "No offense, Sam, but a city kid could spend years in the wilderness and still not learn half of what there is to know."

Just then Joe heard a loud rustling up the slope. He glanced at the others, but no one else seemed to have noticed it. Hoping to spot a bear this time, he said casually, "There's a little creek over there. I'm going to cool off."

Joe made his way through the underbrush. A moment later he called, "Paul, come here!"

The others hurried over to the creek. Joe pointed through the trees at a moose galloping down the slope of the mountain. The creature was larger than any moose Joe had seen pictured. Running through the forest, it was as graceful as a deer.

"Wow. And look over there!" Alex cried, pointing farther to the right. Following Alex's gaze, Joe spotted a small herd of white Dall sheep bolting downhill almost as fast as the moose. Then a black bear scrambled down twenty yards from the hikers.

"What's going on?" Barbara demanded, her eyes raised to a sky suddenly full of birds.

Joe looked up, too. Floating through the air were what looked like long black flies, an inch or two in length. Their tips were red.

"What are these—fireflies?" Joe asked as he caught one. "Ouch! They're hot!"

Paul caught one too. He blew on the tip, which glowed an even brighter red. "Uh-oh," Paul said, suddenly very concerned. "These aren't fireflies. They're singed pine needles. We've got to get out of here. Now!"

Frank glanced up the slope. Black smoke had just mushroomed over the top of the next ridge.

"It's a forest fire!" Sam yelled. "Run!"

"Don't panic," Paul said in a firm, loud voice. He put a hand on Sam's shoulder. "We can't go straight down—the fire would overtake us. We'll have to outflank it."

"How?" Barbara asked, staring up at the smoke and backing away. Alex, who had asthma, had removed an inhaler from his backpack and was pumping it into his mouth.

"We'll cross the creek and move around to the north face of the mountain." Paul had to raise his voice over the increasing noise of frightened animals. "Wonder Lake's at the foot of the mountain. If we can make it to the water we'll be safe, no matter how hot it gets."

"We'd better start now," Joe said, staring at the top of the ridge. Orange fire and black smoke were now rising into the sky, above and to their left. Already, the temperature where the hikers stood was up.

"Let's go," Paul said, pushing his way to the head of the group. "Move it!"

Frank and Joe started running after Paul, jumping the narrow creek and continuing around the wide, steep slope. Glancing over his shoulder, Frank marveled at how normal the spruce and aspens looked just mere feet in front of the roaring, rushing blaze. If trees could talk, he thought, they'd be screaming.

"Up this way!" Paul steered the group uphill, through sparser forest. Frank guessed that the steep climb would take them above the timberline. Paul must hope they'd be safer where there were no trees to feed the fire.

Just then Frank heard a noise like wind rushing through the trees, only lower, more like the growling of a dog.

Paul stopped about twenty feet ahead. Smoke was wafting toward them from the trees in front of them. "The wind has changed!" Paul shouted.

Joe peered through the cloud of smoke now billowing down the mountain. The slope was now engulfed by the spreading fiery blanket. He felt his skin start to heat up.

Paul slapped Joe on the back. "Quit watching, Joe! Run! It's coming after us!"

Joe took off after Frank and the others while Paul brought up the rear.

Frank started to cough as smoke closed in around him, burning his lungs and stinging his eyes. It was hard to see through the growing haze. Tears blurred his vision and streamed down his cheeks. He gasped for air, realizing the air wasn't just harder to breathe—there was less of it. It felt as if the fire was sucking all the oxygen out of the forest!

Joe heard a thump behind him. Alex had slipped and fallen on the rocky ground. When the skinny teenager tumbled again, Joe pulled him to his feet.

Then Paul's booming voice cut through the smoke. "Keep moving! We have to make it to the top of that ridge!" he said, pointing.

Frank took off, hunched over so far that his knees almost hit him in the chest when he ran.

The ridge was so thick with smoke that Frank didn't notice when he had reached the top. He figured it out when he started slipping down on the other side. His lungs burned with every breath he took.

Below was Wonder Lake, a welcome sight. Frank stared off to the left of the lake. Moving along the shore was another fire!

Barbara and Sam scrambled down to join Frank. Then came Joe and Alex. Alex was wheezing even louder than before, and he was standing only because Joe was holding him up.

Paul was last and quickly surveyed the situation. "I can't believe this!" he rasped. "We've got fires coming from behind us and from the side."

Frank pointed to the south end of the lake. "There's a dock over there with a few canoes. Maybe we should head for it."

Paul nodded. "Good. You lead and I'll bring up the rear."

Burning smoke caught up to them after Frank had led the group downhill into the trees. Then came a roar from two hundred yards away followed by heat so intense a tree exploded into a cloud of sparks like a roman candle on the Fourth of July.

Frank saw the dock from a small clearing. It was still a long sprint away. "Let's hurry!" Frank yelled.

Before the group could reach the lake, the fire had swallowed up the tall pines near its shore. Frank realized something that filled him with dread—they would have to go *through* the fire to reach the dock now!

"That way!" Paul hollered, catching up to Frank. He pointed at a clump of burning trees about thirty yards in front of them. Flames whipped between the trees like angry dust devils, but there was a small opening, just large enough for them to push through. On the other side was the lake.

Frank went first, feeling the hair on the back of his neck singe as he passed through the opening. He stopped to wait for the others. It was impossible to see through the swirling, searing smoke. A cluster of shapes darted out of the fire, and Frank heard Paul's voice boom out, "Keep moving!"

Frank staggered down onto the dock, and the others quickly caught up with him—but there were only three of them. Alex was missing—and so was Joe!

Joe knew Alex could never make it on his own. The boy could barely stand, so Joe dragged him through the narrow opening in the wall of fire. They stumbled and fell onto the narrow strip of sand at the forest's edge. Alex's wheezing was louder than ever as he frantically tried to take in lungfuls of air.

Joe scrambled to his feet and lifted Alex by the armpits. "Come on," Joe urged. "It's just a little farther."

Joe and Alex hobbled toward the dock where they could see Barbara and Sam climbing into an aluminum canoe with Paul. Frank ran back down the dock toward his brother, but Joe waved him back. "Get in the canoe and get ready to shove off!" he shouted.

Joe felt the dock wobble as he stepped onto it,

supporting Alex. Alex could barely move, from trying so hard to breathe. Without warning, something at the edge of the sandy strip exploded with a loud *whoompf*. Joe whipped his head around to watch as a towering evergreen exploded into flames.

Joe's blue eyes widened in horror. The huge tree wasn't just burning, it was also falling—straight at them. If it didn't crush them, it would burn them alive!

Chapter
2

"Jump!" Joe shouted, shoving Alex into the lake. Joe didn't even wait for Alex to hit the water before he followed. A thunderous crash filled his ears as the cold water engulfed him.

Joe grabbed Alex underwater and surfaced with him in a swirl of blazing branches and splintered boards. The massive old evergreen hissed in the buckled wreckage of the dock. An empty canoe floated past. Joe clutched it with one hand and held Alex above water with the other.

Frank dove out of his canoe and swam over to help. Minutes later the boys had clambered into the canoe. As soon as they were safely in the boat, Joe grabbed the inhaler from Alex's jacket pocket and forced it into his hand. Automatically, Alex pumped the inhaler into his mouth and breathed deeply.

11

"Are you okay?" Joe asked anxiously.

"Yeah," Alex rasped. "Just need to get out of here."

Frank shook his head. "One minute we're breathing fresh mountain air, and the next minute we're choking on it," he murmured to his brother.

Joe nodded. He plucked the only paddle out of the bottom of the boat while Frank reached for a piece of wood that would make a half-decent oar.

As the brothers started paddling away from shore, Joe watched Paul in the other canoe, staring at the shore, now bright orange with fire.

"What's the matter, Paul?" Joe called out. "We're safe now, right?"

"Oh, sure," Paul responded, picking up an oar. "We just row to the far side of the lake. After that, it's a two-mile hike to Kantishna campground. We can catch a shuttle bus out of the park from there. But it looks like our trek is finished."

"Can't we hike somewhere else?" Barbara asked, picking up the other oar to help Paul.

Paul shook his head. "This fire is too big. The park service won't issue any more back-country permits until they're sure it's completely out."

Frank glanced back to see flames leaping from tree to tree. "How do you think it got started?"

"I don't know," Paul replied. "Most fires around here are caused by lightning. But we haven't had a thunderstorm in over two months. We had a dry winter, too. The park's parched."

"Maybe someone left a campfire burning," Joe suggested.

Paul nodded. "That's always a possibility. But we've had nearly a dozen major fires in the park so far this summer. Word's getting out that it's dangerous here this year. Tourism's slacked off a lot, which means my business is down."

Joe heard a new sound over the dull roar of the fire. He raised his eyes to see a plane flying over the fire on the west side of the lake. He was startled to see yellow-clad figures jumping out of the plane, parachutes popping open a few seconds later.

"They're jumping into the fire!" Joe yelled.

"Of course. They're smoke jumpers," Paul said. "Fire fighters with parachutes."

"They jump *into* the fire?" Joe asked, still amazed. "How do they keep from getting burned up?"

"They don't really jump into it," Paul replied. "They just try to get as close as possible so they won't have a long hike to it. They usually land about a half mile away."

"How'd they get there so fast?" Sam asked from the middle of his canoe.

"Spotters," Paul explained. "You've seen those big wooden towers? Spotters spend all day scanning the forest with binoculars in those. When they see smoke, they call it in. An hour later, you might see a plane fly over and drop flame-smothering chemicals. Then the smoke jumpers move in."

When they reached the far shore and got out, Paul pointed north. "We're going that way. We've still got a fire behind us, so don't stop to measure any bear prints. You okay, Alex?"

"Much better, thanks." Alex managed a rueful grin. "This sure has been a more exciting trek than I signed up for."

The group headed north. Half an hour later Frank noticed dark clouds moving in. He heard the rumble of distant thunder. "It looks like a storm's on its way," he said to Paul.

"Just in time," Paul said with relief. "Maybe the rain will help contain the fire."

It was pouring when the trekkers reached Kantishna campground that evening. The campground was deserted. Paul guessed that the campers had been warned of the fire. As they all climbed aboard the last bus of the day, Paul told them that the park entrance was three hours away. Frank and Joe each settled into a backseat on the bus and fell asleep, exhausted.

A couple hours later the bus hit a bump and jostled Frank awake. He glanced at his watch. It was after ten. Daylight at ten o'clock? Then Frank remembered how far north they were. The sun was up twenty hours a day in Denali Park. Sunset would be around midnight.

Frank looked out the window. The rain had

stopped, and the bus was now moving through high, flat tundra. Frank saw a herd of bull caribou with huge racks of antlers moving over the land. It was a marvelous sight.

All the others were asleep, except Paul, who was sitting in front of Frank.

Paul was staring out the window, sitting very still. Frank leaned forward and tapped him on the elbow. "Is something wrong, Paul?"

Paul turned around, then sighed. "I was just thinking about how sudden that fire was."

"Right," Frank said, moving up into the empty seat next to Paul. "Back at the lake you said that careless campers might have started it. But you didn't sound convinced."

"Where are we?" Joe murmured, half asleep.

"Almost at the park entrance," Frank told him. "Paul and I were talking about the fire."

Joe was instantly awake. "So what *do* you think started it, Paul?"

Paul turned so he could look at both Frank and Joe. "Can you keep a secret?"

Frank and Joe nodded in unison.

Paul scratched at some dirt on his hiking shorts. "There have been ten big fires in Denali since the end of May—eleven counting the one today. That's an unusually high number for this area, even when the forest is incredibly dry. After the third fire, I started plotting the locations on a map, along with an estimate of when they started. I was hoping to avoid hiking in a danger zone."

Paul hesitated, looking from Joe to Paul. "Out of eleven fires, seven have started near one of my treks. This is the seventh time I've had to pull a group out of the mountains and cancel a week of trekking."

"Let me get this straight," Joe said. "You're saying that no matter where you hike, chances are good that a fire will start there?"

Paul nodded. "Weird, huh?"

The bus pulled into the visitors' center parking lot a little after eleven that night. Paul made a few calls from a pay phone, and then the exhausted trekkers piled into the back of his dark blue pickup truck.

"We're in luck," Paul said to Frank and Joe, who won the toss to ride in the cab with him. "I found a place for you guys to spend the night. The Eagle's Nest Lodge has a few rooms available. It's only about half a mile up the highway."

The Eagle's Nest was a huge one-story log cabin with a lobby filled with leather furniture and hunting trophies. On the walls hung deer, elk, moose, and caribou heads. A stuffed nine-foot grizzly reared up beside the flagstone fireplace, and a rather moth-eaten black bear guarded the picture window.

It was a big but cozy room, lit only by a single lamp at the front desk and by flickering flames from the fireplace. The room smelled of smoke from the burning logs. Joe had to remind himself that sometimes the smell of smoke did *not* signal danger.

"Hey, Paul," someone called. "I see you guys got out alive."

Joe turned. A young woman was moving out from behind the front desk. She had shoulder-length blond hair, brown eyes, and dimples in her cheeks. She wore jeans and a denim work shirt.

"Hi, Sandy," Paul said. "We got out, but just barely. Everybody, meet the manager of the Eagle's Nest." Paul introduced Sandy to Barbara, Sam, Alex, Frank, and Joe. Joe wondered if it was his imagination or if Sandy gave him and Frank an especially warm smile.

"How'd you guys survive the fire?" she asked.

Joe grinned. "We ran real fast."

Paul gave her a quick summary of how they had escaped the flames at Wonder Lake. "So what's the latest?" he asked her. "Have they got the fire under control yet?"

"Almost," Sandy said. "The rain helped. I called the Bureau of Land Management an hour ago, and they said the smoke jumpers had just about finished the line."

"What line?" Alex asked.

"A trench they dig around the fire," Sandy explained. "It stops the fire from spreading.

"They had to dig a long one this time," she

added. "The fire's already spread over a thousand acres."

"Is that big?" Frank asked.

"Big enough," Paul responded. "Some fires here this summer have been even bigger."

Sandy gestured toward the couches in front of the fireplace. "Do you want to unwind a bit or go straight to bed?" she asked. They decided to sit and relax for a while.

Tired and sore, they slumped into the comfortable leather chairs and sofas set in a circle around the fireplace.

"Is it really over for us, Paul?" Barbara asked, her pretty face smudged with soot.

Paul sighed. "I'll call the ranger's office tomorrow to make sure, but I don't see any way the trek can continue. What I'm worried about now is that this fire could close me up for the rest of the month."

Sam cleared his throat. "I hate to sound greedy, but we signed up for a week, and now it's over on the first day of trekking—"

"You'll get your money back, Sam," Paul said, standing up to go. Then he continued, "I'll stop by tomorrow morning to let you know what's going on. For now, get a good night's rest—and be grateful we all got out alive."

"Wait," Frank said, following Paul to the door. "I was wondering," he continued in a low voice out of the others' hearing, "could Joe and I have a look at that map you told us about?"

Paul studied Frank for a moment. "Okay," he said. "I don't see why not. Now, do you mean?"

Joe, who had joined them, suggested, "Maybe we could, uh, grab a burger or pizza or something before taking off."

Paul grinned. "I've got food," he said. "How do you like your steak, Joe?"

A smile broke over Joe's sooty face. "Right *now*—and with lots of meat on it!"

Moments later the Hardys were once again bouncing along in Paul's pickup, this time on a rocky one-lane road. On the right, the ground fell away to a boulder-strewn creekbed fifty feet below. Frank rolled down his window and saw the truck's tires speeding along only inches from the edge.

"You know, it's funny," said Joe, who was sitting between Frank and Paul. "You say most forest fires are caused by lightning, but there hasn't been any lightning here lately. On the other hand, seven out of eleven fires have started near where you were hiking. Is there any chance that a person could have set those fires on purpose? Someone who didn't like you?"

Paul's gaze flicked from the road to Joe and back again.

"For a couple of teenagers from Bayport, you guys sure are curious," he said.

"We know," Frank spoke up. "Maybe you've

heard of our dad—Fenton Hardy, the detective. We've helped him out on cases lots of times."

"Detectives, huh?" Paul acted both surprised and amused. "I thought you guys might be smarter than you looked. As a matter of fact, I have been thinking about who might have wanted to set fires in these mountains. The only person I could come up with was—"

Paul was interrupted by a muffled pop, followed quickly by a much louder boom.

"What's going on?" Paul exclaimed as the truck slid sideways. He grappled with the steering wheel, but the truck continued to careen wildly, skirting dangerously close to the edge of the cliff.

"It's a blowout!" Frank cried, glancing at the cliff to his right.

"It's no use—I can't hold it!" Paul yelled. "Hang on! We're going over!"

Chapter

3

"HANG ON!" PAUL SHOUTED.

Sitting between Frank and Paul, Joe didn't have much to hang on to except the seat cushion, and his fingers had already ripped the worn fabric.

Paul slammed on the brakes, and the truck skidded to the right. Joe felt a hard jolt and knew the rear tire had gone off the edge. Paul jerked the steering wheel to the left. The truck bucked and groaned, and the tire bounced back onto the roadway.

"Look out!" Joe screamed as the truck veered sharply to the left and a large spruce tree loomed in the windshield. He threw his hands out to brace for the impact if his seat belt didn't hold.

The truck smashed into the tree, and Joe's hands smacked into the padded dashboard, his arms taking the full impact. Before the dust had a chance to settle, Paul had hit his door handle and jumped out of the truck.

"Are you all right?" Frank asked, putting a hand on Joe's shoulder.

Joe groaned. "I'm alive and nothing's broken. So I guess I can't complain."

"Sure you could," Frank responded with a slight grin. "But nobody would listen."

Paul hollered, from behind the truck, "This tire is flatter than a pancake. I must have run over something that punched a hole in it."

Frank and Joe got out and walked to the back of the truck, where Paul was poking at the shredded left rear tire. Frank didn't stop to look at the tire. He kept walking back up the road, his eyes scanning the hillside near the road.

"What are you looking for?" Joe called out to his brother.

"Somebody took a shot at us," Frank replied. "I'm sure I heard a gunshot just before the tire blew out."

Frank hiked along the hillside for about fifty yards and stopped at a clump of juniper bushes. He walked slowly around the bushes and then headed back to the truck.

"There were some footprints behind those bushes," Frank reported. His gaze settled on Paul. "If I were going to set up an ambush for somebody coming down this road, that would be a pretty good spot."

"This has gone too far!" Paul burst out, kicking the flat tire. "I've had it with that woman!"

Joe glanced at Frank. "What woman?" he asked.

"The one who probably took a shot at us," Paul said. "My ex-girlfriend, Rose Hudiburg."

"I guess you decided not to be friends," Joe remarked.

"I can't believe her!" Paul raged. "We could've been killed!"

Frank knelt down by the flat tire and took a closer look at it. He pulled out his pocketknife and began digging into the deflated rubber. A few seconds later he pulled out a thin metal slug with a blunted tip.

Frank held the bullet up. "Looks like a twenty-two," he said, handing it to Paul. "Does Rose own a gun?"

"Sure," Paul answered. "She's a ranger."

Joe stared at him. "A park ranger took a shot at us?"

"You might have seen her at the park entrance this morning," Paul said. "Remember all those people packing into a bus, going on the wildlife tour? She was the ranger driving the bus."

Joe remembered the woman with short brown hair and long legs. "You broke up with her? Why?"

"Money," Paul said. "One hundred thousand dollars, to be exact."

"Hold on a second," Frank said. "Tell us what you mean."

"Have you ever heard of SRO Corporation?" Frank responded.

"Sure," Frank said. "They own a movie studio, a couple of amusement parks, and a bunch of hotels across the country."

"Well, I guess that isn't enough for them," Paul said. "Now they want the concession rights to Denali Park so they can build a new hotel and restaurants here.

"And they've got enough money to make it happen," he continued. "They paid Rose a hundred grand to spy on their competitor for the concession rights, a guy named Jeff Rankin. Rankin owns a lodge in Talkeetna. He's tough and a real go-getter. He has a sideline selling 'disaster' souvenirs to tourists. When that big oil tanker foundered off the Alaska coastline, Rankin sold tanker paperweights at his lodge. He made a fortune off stuffed gray whales after three real whales got trapped under the Barrow ice. This year I hear he's already manufacturing T-shirts with pictures of smoke jumpers and sayings like 'I survived the Denali National Park fires.'"

Paul paused, glanced at his pickup, and peered up and down the gravel road. "We might as well hike back to the lodge. It's closer than my cabin, and I don't think we'll be able to hitch a ride at this time of night."

"What did Rose dig up on Rankin?" Frank asked as the three of them started back.

"She found out how much his bid was," Paul

answered. "Then SRO came in with a lower bid and won. Those concession rights are worth five, maybe six million dollars a year."

"What does all of this have to do with you?" Joe asked.

"Rose told me about the payoff," Paul answered. "She even showed me the money she got from SRO. She wanted to use it to help me expand Bull Moose Treks. That way we'd be partners, she said. And we could get married with the money the business would make."

He kicked a rock off the road. "I guess she also figured she was doing the world a favor by making sure Rankin didn't get his hooks into Denali. But it just didn't seem right to me. I told her that accepting that money was wrong, and I didn't want anything to do with it—or her."

"I guess she didn't take it well," Joe said.

"I guess not," Paul muttered.

"But do you really think she'd shoot at you?" Joe asked Paul.

Paul frowned. "She has a temper. One time she threw a broom at me when I dropped a jar of pickles on her kitchen floor."

Frank was skeptical. "Can you think of anyone else who might have a grudge against you?"

"No one," Paul responded miserably. "Believe me, since these fires started I've searched my memory. The thing is, I spend most of my time hiking in the mountains. I haven't made that many friends around here, much less enemies."

Frank glanced at his brother. "Looks like another working vacation," he said.

"Fine with me," Joe replied easily. "As long as there's food at the end of the road."

Paul was able to talk Sandy out of some leftovers from the Eagle's Nest kitchen. After eating, Frank and Joe fell into bed for a few hours' sleep. In the morning they called their parents to let them know they were all right. Barbara and Alex were in the lobby, in line with a dozen other guests waiting to check out.

"Where are you guys going?" Joe asked them.

"The airline says we can't fly to the Midwest until the weekend, so we thought we'd go watch the salmon run at Brooks Falls," Alex said. "Sam left early this morning for Denver, though."

"We're not going to see the salmon, though, we're going to see the bears," Barbara added. "They come to catch the fish as they swim upstream."

Joe spotted Paul coming through the front door. "Hey, Paul!" he called out, walking over to meet him. "Why don't you join us for breakfast?"

"I could use some food," Paul replied. "It's been a long morning already. I hitched a ride into Healy because I wanted to talk to the sheriff in person about the shooting."

"Did you tell the sheriff about Rose?" Frank asked, coming up behind Joe.

Paul shook his head. "I want to talk to her first. As soon as my truck is fixed, I'll track her down."

Joe heard voices outside. He peered out the window and saw four men climb out of a van and head for the lodge. They were wearing hard hats, green pants, and yellow shirts blackened by soot and ash. Joe guessed that they were the smoke jumpers.

The men strode into the lobby and fell into the couches and chairs near where the Hardys and Paul were standing. They looked as if they hadn't slept in days.

"I'm going to call the garage about my truck," Paul said to the Hardys. "I'll meet you guys in the dining room."

"And I'm going to call the park service," Frank said to Joe as Paul walked away. "I want to find out if Rose was working last night."

Joe stayed in the lobby, keeping an eye on the grimy smoke jumpers. One of them got up and started past Joe.

"Excuse me," Joe said as the man passed. "Are you a smoke jumper?"

The man paused, grinned modestly, and extended his hand. He was at least a head shorter than Joe. "You bet. I'm Dave Ahshapanek."

Joe clasped his hand. "Joe Hardy. I'm sorry, what was your last name?"

"It's Indian, Kiowa people," Ahshapanek ex-

27

plained. "The guys in the crew just call me Rocky."

"So you're one of the guys who put that blaze out last night," Joe said.

Rocky grinned. "There's no way to kill a monster that size in just one night, kid. It'll keep smoldering and flaring up for weeks. But we managed to turn it into a ten o'clock fire, with a little help from the rain."

"A ten o'clock fire?" Joe asked.

"That's a fire you get under control by ten in the morning the day after you jump," Rocky said. "When you work with Homer Dodge, most fires are ten o'clocks. He works fast."

Rocky pointed at a man with a red flattop haircut and a thick mustache. "Homer's the best foreman in the business, if you ask me."

Joe studied the older man. Dodge had one leg swung over the edge of the couch. He was telling a joke to the other two smoke jumpers. When he got to the punch line, he laughed so hard Joe thought he would fall off the couch.

"He seems to be a born storyteller," Joe remarked.

"Yeah—Homer's a story in himself," Rocky said. "You've never seen such a Sherlock when the heat is on. He disappeared for about three hours at the fire yesterday. We thought he might be hurt or something and were making plans to save him. Then he turns up all of a sudden and says, 'Go that way.' We go, and a few minutes later the place where we were standing is toast."

Rocky shook his head in admiration. "Too bad he has to quit," he continued. "He turns forty this year. The Bureau of Land Management doesn't let you jump past that age."

When Frank came back from using the phone, Joe introduced him to Rocky, who then took the brothers over to the couch where Dodge was sitting. "Homer, meet Frank and Joe Hardy," Rocky said. "They were running from the fire yesterday when we jumped."

Dodge stood up and shook their hands. Joe thought he had a grip like a vise. "Pleasure to see you're still alive," Dodge said in a gruff voice. "That was some fire."

Dodge introduced the Hardys to the other two members of his crew: his craggy-faced, huge assistant, Morley Willis, and Jim Carroll, a wavy-haired schoolteacher from Washington.

Joe smiled in admiration. "Your work seems kind of, well, scary."

The foreman nodded. "It is. But all smoke jumpers are a little bit crazy, you know. Nobody in his right mind would jump into a fire with nothing for protection except a shovel."

"I must be crazy, too, then," Joe said, "because it sounds like fun to me. Where are you guys based?"

"Fairbanks," Dodge said. "We're headed back as soon as our chopper gets here."

"I don't suppose you'd have room for a couple of trainees," Joe ventured. "Our vacation plans went up in smoke."

Dodge chuckled, then eyed the Hardys sharply. "Are you serious?" he asked Joe. "You two want to try smoke jumping?"

Frank looked at his brother in alarm. "Wait a minute. I thought we had stuff to do here."

"We can still take care of that," Joe said, knowing that Frank was referring to Paul's suspicions and the mystery they might solve. "But we're supposed to be having fun, right? And the hiking trip did fall through."

Dodge put his hands in his back pockets. "Sounds good to me," he said with a grin. "We can always use more volunteers in a fire season like this. Why don't you two ride in the chopper to Fairbanks with us? You can take the train back here later."

Joe checked with Frank, who finally nodded. "That sounds great!" Joe said to Dodge, smiling.

Dodge waved goodbye as the Hardys walked toward the dining hall. Frank wondered if the charismatic man had ever hypnotized anyone with his eyes.

At breakfast Frank told Joe that, according to the park service, Rose hadn't worked the night before.

"So that makes her a suspect, right?" Joe said.

"Our *only* suspect," Frank corrected him.

Joe saw Paul walking into the dining hall. Joe stood up, waving to get Paul's attention. Then he noticed that someone was approaching Paul from behind—a man in a state trooper's uniform.

As Joe watched, the state trooper caught up with Paul and asked, "Are you Paul Garcia?"

Paul eyed the officer warily, then nodded.

"I have a warrant for your arrest, Mr. Garcia." The trooper, a towering man, slapped a pair of handcuffs over Paul's wrists.

The dining room became still as the other guests stared at the officer and his captive. "What's going on?" Joe demanded, storming up to the pair.

"Good question," Paul agreed loudly. He glared at the trooper. "What did I do wrong exactly? Forget to pay a parking ticket?"

The trooper looked around at the room full of people. Then he held up the warrant. "No, sir," he said to Paul. "It's worse than that. I'm charging you with arson."

Chapter

4

"THIS IS CRAZY!" Joe cried, moving between Paul and the state trooper. "Paul didn't—"

"Stand back, son," the trooper said firmly, pushing Joe off to the side.

"You're making a big mista—"

The trooper put his hand on his holster and unsnapped the flap over the top of his revolver. "You're the one making the mistake," the trooper warned Joe. "Step out of the way now. I won't say it again."

Joe stepped out of the way. "What's going on, Paul?" he asked.

Paul shook his head helplessly. "I don't know."

"Officer, I'm a friend of Paul's," Frank said calmly. "Can you tell me why he's being charged with arson? Are you accusing him of setting forest fires?"

As the trooper led Paul down the hall, Paul glanced back over his shoulder at the Hardys and mouthed the words "Find Rose."

The trooper opened the door to a lodge office. "Let's go in here, Mr. Garcia. I'll read you your rights and then you can call a lawyer."

Joe saw Homer Dodge talking with Rocky in the lobby. They had watched as Paul was led down the hall in handcuffs. Joe and Frank ran over to them.

"Homer, do you know why they arrested Paul?" Joe asked him.

Dodge nodded. "The investigators from the Bureau of Land Management found an explosive device about two miles from the lake in an abandoned shack. The park rangers showed us Garcia's permit for your expedition. That's how we knew he went by there yesterday."

"It's not hard to set a fire that way," Rocky added. "You make a bomb with some plastic explosives, attach it to a timer and a dry cell battery, then soak the area with gasoline. Set the timer, leave, and then it goes off and starts a fire."

"But why'd they arrest Paul?" Joe asked. "That explosive device in the shack was never detonated. It can't possibly implicate him in *anything*. It makes no sense."

"He had the opportunity to store a bomb in the shack. No one's saying that's the bomb that set the fire, but only that he might be stockpiling devices for more fires. Also gasoline and timers were found in the back of his truck," Dodge added gravely. "That's pretty strong circumstantial evidence. The sheriff in Healy got a call from the garage when Garcia's truck was in for repairs this morning. They called him about what they had found in the truck because of all the recent forest fires."

"You sure know a lot about this," Frank said.

"I'm on the losing end of any fire, and I want them stopped," Dodge replied. "The investigators put two and two together and I guess they came up with Garcia."

"We had a hard time believing the fire was started by lightning," Joe said. "But it couldn't have been started by Paul. He was with a member of our group at all times. Also, the fire started higher up the mountain than we ever got. He couldn't have sneaked away to start it without one of us knowing he was gone."

"Believe what you want, Joe, but they feel they have enough to hold him," Dodge said. "He could have started it with a remote." Then he shook his head. "A tree hugger who starts forest fires. And I thought I'd seen everything."

The trooper stepped out of the office and asked Dodge to come inside. Dodge walked away, and Rocky stood up. "I'm starving. I'm going to get some chow," Rocky said. "See you guys later."

Frank looked at Joe. "Let's go back to our room," he said.

Joe waited for Frank to shut the door, then said, "I can't believe this!"

"I can't either," Frank said. "None of it fits. The only thing tying Paul to the fire is the stuff found in his truck. Also, why didn't any of our party see that stuff yesterday? If Paul did start the fires, he wouldn't have told us about his map with all the fire locations marked."

"You thinking what I'm thinking? That he was set up?" Joe asked.

"I think it's a good possibility," Frank responded.

"Rose?" Joe ventured.

"I don't know," Frank said, opening his pack. "Why don't you walk to the visitors' center and see if you can find her?"

"Okay," Joe said. "What are you looking for?"

Frank pulled out the pair of jeans he had worn the day before. He dug into one of the pockets. "This," he said, holding up the bullet he had dug out of Paul's tire. "I'll walk partway with you to that sporting goods store that we passed on the road."

"The Sure Shot?" Joe responded.

"Right. I want to find out the caliber of this slug."

"You think the shooting last night might be connected to Paul's arrest?" Joe asked.

"You know how I hate coincidences," Frank answered. "Paul thinks Rose took a shot at us last night. Now he's been arrested for arson. It's possible that if she couldn't get him one way, she'd try something else. So we need to see if we can trace that bullet to her."

Joe nodded. "Let's meet back here for lunch."

When Frank walked into the Sure Shot, he heard voices coming from an office at the back of the store. He ambled back that way, past the aisles of day packs, canteens, guns, and camouflage hunting clothes. When he got to lanterns and stoves, Frank began to make out what the voices were saying.

"You make a lot of money off my T-shirts," a gruff voice said. "It'd be a real shame if you lost that revenue."

"I'll take my chances, Jeff," another man answered. "We used to have a good deal, the same deal I get on all the other shirts I sell—fifty percent. Now you want me to settle for thirty-five."

Frank wondered if "Jeff" was Jeff Rankin, the Talkeetna lodge owner and T-shirt king. He moved closer to hear better.

"You're passing up a big opportunity," Jeff said. "These shirts are the hottest thing in Alaska since the Tok River fire. I'll make a special deal just for you. Thirty-seven percent—that's my final offer."

"You call that a deal? I think I'll pass. You're

not the only guy who knows how to print clever words and pretty pictures on T-shirts. I think I'll stick to the safe ones like 'I survived the Alaska Highway' and 'I climbed Mount McKinley and all I got for it was this stupid T-shirt.' "

"Have it your way," Jeff responded. "But you may live to regret that decision."

A man came out of the office, dressed in faded jeans, cowboy boots, and a black T-shirt that said "I survived the Moosecreek fire." He headed straight down the aisle and out the front door. He hopped into a red pickup truck. Frank didn't think he'd have any problem remembering the license plate: HOT SHIRTS.

Shortly after that the other man came out of the office. "Can I help you?" he said when he saw Frank.

Frank pulled the bullet out of his pocket. "Can you tell me what kind of bullet this is? I found it out in the woods the other day. It looks like a twenty-two, but I wanted to make sure."

The man walked over to Frank, put on his glasses and took the bullet to examine it. He held it up to the light, then gave it back to Frank. "You're right, it's a twenty-two. I almost felt like putting one of these between the eyes of that guy that just walked out of here."

"Was that Jeff Rankin, the T-shirt guy?"

The man smiled. "The one and only. He'd cook his mother in a microwave if he could get a T-shirt out of it. I'm Dick Stout," the man said.

He smiled and held out his hand to Frank. "I own this place."

"Frank Hardy." Then Frank handed him the bullet again. "Out of curiosity, can you tell if this bullet was shot by a rifle or a pistol?"

Stout examined it again. "It could've been fired by any number of weapons. A twenty-two rifle, pistol, a—"

Stout stopped abruptly. Frank noticed that Stout was gazing intently at a shelf behind him. Frank turned to look at the shelf full of cook stoves and lanterns. The lanterns were moving.

The lanterns wiggled gently for a few seconds, then everything on the shelf started moving and making noise. Guns in the racks behind Stout looked as if they were trying to break through the metal bar holding them in. A lamp on the glass display case began to rock on its base. The sound of metal and glass rattled throughout the store.

Then Frank felt the floor begin to shimmy.

Stout grabbed Frank by the arm. "We get shocks like this all the time. Have you ever been in an earthqua—"

Stout was cut off by a loud crash as the front plate-glass window exploded, sending a deadly shower of razor-sharp glass shards hurtling through the store.

Chapter

5

FRANK DUCKED behind the display counter with the lamp, yanking Stout down with him as glass shards whizzed past, just inches over their heads. A fragment the size of Frank's hand whirled across the store and buried itself into the head of a camouflage-clad mannequin.

Then the rumbling faded, and the rattling died down as the camping gear stopped dancing off the shelves. An eerie silence filled the store.

"That one was bigger than usual," Stout said, getting up and surveying the damage.

"Usual?" Frank responded. "Do you have a lot of earthquakes around here?"

Stout shrugged. "We get our share. Most of them are just microshocks that you barely feel."

Stout got a broom and dustpan out of a store-room and started sweeping up glass.

"You have a big selection of T-shirts," Frank noted. "Do you sell a lot of them?"

Stout chuckled. "I'll be selling a lot less now. Rankin's shirts are popular, but he's too greedy. He thinks he can bully anybody into doing business his way. I don't like being bullied."

Frank helped Stout sweep up most of the glass before he left.

"Don't catch any more bullets," Stout called as Frank walked out the door.

It didn't take Joe long to find Rose Hudiburg at the visitors' center. A ranger at the front desk pointed out her office, and Joe found her alone in a room with three drab gray-metal desks. She was sitting at the middle desk—a small woman with a deep tan, brown hair, and brown eyes.

Joe introduced himself as he stepped in the door. "We have a mutual friend," he said. "Paul Garcia. He told me to come see you."

Rose leaned back in her chair and clasped her hands in front of her. Joe thought she looked older than Paul and guessed she was at least thirty.

"Paul sent you?" she said. "Why?"

Sitting down in the chair facing her desk, Joe told Rose what had happened to Paul.

Rose frowned. "Why are you telling me this?"

"Maybe you know something that could clear him," Joe said.

Rose studied her desktop for a few seconds. "You know Paul and I broke up," she said.

"He told me," Joe said.

Rose stood up and walked to the window behind her desk. Mount McKinley loomed in the distance, framing her head.

"I couldn't care less about Paul now," Rose said.

Joe didn't believe her. She was trying too hard to convince him.

"But he's no arsonist," she added. "You should be looking for a man named Jeff Rankin."

"They guy who owns the lodge at Talkeetna?" Joe asked.

"He's the logical choice," Rose said. "Paul's a nature-lover. He wouldn't start a forest fire. Rankin, though, has reasons. Forest fires are good for T-shirt sales, for one thing. He's got to make the mortgage payments on his big house in Moody. Plus, he's mad about losing a business deal a while back, and starting fires in the park would be a good way to get revenge for that."

"I heard about that concession business deal," Joe said. He waited a few seconds before dropping his bombshell. "In fact, I heard you had something to do with that—and that you were paid well for your cooperation."

Rose glared at him. "Who told you that?"

"Who do you think?" Joe responded.

Rose turned to look out the window. She crossed her arms and took a deep breath. "I was going to use the money to help Paul expand his business. We talked about getting married." She pivoted back to Joe, tears welling in the corners of her eyes. "But none of that matters anymore. I gave the money back."

Joe looked away for a few seconds, not proud of reducing Rose to tears. Then he said, "So why'd they arrest Paul?"

Rose pulled a tissue out of a desk drawer and wiped her eyes. She took a few seconds to collect herself, then stared at Joe. "I don't know," she said. "This is the first I've heard about it. You probably know more than I do."

Joe wanted to believe her—but he saw something on her desk that made him skeptical.

A small nylon waist pack lay open on the metal cabinet beside her desk. Joe caught a glint of something shiny inside—the glint of a steel barrel.

"Do rangers ever carry guns?" Joe asked her.

The question caught Rose off guard. "Only in emergencies," she said. "Some have shotguns in their trucks."

Joe jabbed a finger at the waist pack. "So what is that?" he asked angrily.

Rose snatched up her pack. "What I carry in here is none of your business."

"It is now," Joe snapped. "Last night we were driving to Paul's cabin, and someone put a bullet in his tire."

42

Rose gave Joe an incredulous stare. "You think I did that?"

Joe stood up, glaring back at her. "Do you lead nature tours with a gun in your purse?"

Rose reached into the bag and whipped out the small pistol. "I use this to scare bears away. Lots of people in Alaska have guns to scare bears away."

She thrust the gun back in the pack. "And to scare away people like you. Now get out of here!"

By lunchtime the fire had scared off most of the guests at the Eagle's Nest. Frank and Joe were the only ones eating lunch in the dining hall.

Joe swallowed a bite of his burger, then told Frank what had happened at the visitors' center.

"For what it's worth," Joe added, "Rose said Rankin's the one we should be looking for."

"I found him," Frank said. He told Joe about the argument he overheard at the Sure Shot and wiped his mouth with his napkin. "Rankin talked like a tough character. He might use a gun to get what he wants. But right now we don't have any evidence linking him to the shooting or the fires."

Their conversation was interrupted by a deep thrumming sound that grew louder and louder.

The Hardys jumped up and ran outside to watch a big, fat helicopter set down in front of the lodge, where Dodge and his crew were standing.

"There you are," Dodge said to the Hardys. "Are you coming?"

The brothers looked at each other. "I don't know," Frank said.

"Oh, by the way, Paul Garcia's coming with us," Dodge said. "We're taking him and the trooper, Officer Haynes."

"Why are they going to Fairbanks?" Joe asked.

"The state troopers' regional office is there," Dodge answered.

Frank checked with Joe, who nodded. "Okay, we're going," Frank said.

"Great. I'll get Haynes and Garcia," Dodge said, strolling off.

Frank glanced at Joe. "We can't do anything more for Paul here," he said. "Maybe we'll learn something about this arson device if we go wi—"

A hand fell on Frank's shoulder. "Homer tells me you boys are tagging along."

Frank turned to face one of the smoke jumpers. He stood about an inch taller than Frank's six one. "You're Willis, right?" Frank asked.

The man nodded. "I'm Homer's assistant."

"Why are we going to Fairbanks in a helicopter?" Frank asked. "You came down here in a plane."

"We do all our jumps out of a DC-Three, but the chopper usually picks us up afterward because it can set down in remote places," Willis explained. "Sometimes we're so far back in the woods that it'd take us two or three days to hike

44

to the nearest airstrip. So the folks at our head-quarters in Fairbanks send a chopper for us."

Frank was amazed by the size of the helicopter, which had two rotors. "Isn't that the same model helicopter the president flies in?" he asked.

Willis nodded. "A C-Stallion, the one you always see touching down on the White House lawn."

Dodge and Rocky came up behind them. "Everybody's ready," Dodge said. "We're flying four crew, three extras, a pilot, and an arsonist."

"A *suspected* arsonist," Frank corrected him.

Dodge shrugged. "Okay, Garcia's innocent until proven guilty. But if I were the jury, he'd be on his way to prison right now."

Rocky shook his head slowly. "I can't believe it. We were eating smoke all day because of a nature-lover who starts forest fires? Let's take him on our next jump and shove him out the hatch without a chute."

Frank heard shouting over the drone of the helicopter engines. He turned and saw a short man in aviator glasses and a baseball cap arguing with Jeff Rankin. Rankin was trying to walk away from the helicopter, but the short man was standing in his way, butting up against Rankin as he pushed forward.

Dodge ran over and caught the shorter man around the shoulders as he took a swing at Rankin. Rankin strutted away, laughing, and the shorter man headed for the helicopter. Dodge walked back over to the Hardys.

"What was that all about?" Frank asked.

"Two men who hate each other's guts," Dodge said. "Jeff Rankin and Albert Brunner. Al's our chopper pilot. He lost a lot of money to Rankin in a card game last year."

"What was Rankin doing here now?" Joe asked.

"He flew choppers in the army," Dodge replied. "He probably just wanted to take a peek at the big bird."

Frank told Dodge about the scene between Rankin and Stout at the Sure Shot that morning.

Dodge whistled. "Money makes people do crazy things, doesn't it?"

Paul, hands cuffed behind his back, stared at the Hardys as he and the trooper boarded the helicopter. But Trooper Haynes wouldn't let Frank or Joe talk to Paul. Haynes and the trek leader took the passenger seats behind the cockpit. The Hardys sat on a bench along the side with Dodge and the crew.

About halfway through the hour flight to Fairbanks, Joe asked Rocky a question.

"What's it like, working for Homer?"

Rocky grinned. "For one thing, you learn that you're tougher than you think you are," he said, almost yelling to be heard over the whirling rotors. "If you tell Homer you're tired, he says you're not that tired. If you tell him you're hurt, Homer says you're not that hurt. He'll make you tougher than a cheap steak. You eat a lot of smoke and dig a lot of fire lines when you jump with him. But that's what it takes to join the club."

"What club?" Joe asked.

"This club right here," Rocky said. "We're like the Green Berets of fire fighters."

Rocky winked, then leaned back against the wall of the chopper and closed his eyes. Joe saw Dodge reading a magazine on the other side of the chopper and moved across to talk to him.

"How long have you been doing this?" Joe asked, shouting over the chopper's noise.

"All my life," Dodge yelled back. "But this was probably my last fire."

"What do you mean?" Joe asked.

Dodge shrugged. "You have to be young, tough, and lucky to be a smoke jumper. I'm still tough and lucky—but I'm not young anymore."

Suddenly the engine started to sputter. Dodge whirled toward the cockpit. "What's wrong, Al?"

The pilot leaned forward and fiddled with the throttle controls, muttering to himself. The engine coughed some more.

Frank peered through a window and saw a stream of fuel pouring out of the engine. "We've got a leak!" he shouted. "It's coming down the side!"

The engine coughed, sputtered, and died. A deathly silence filled the cabin. Then the chopper began to fall like a rock.

Chapter

6

JOE STARED WIDE-EYED as the helicopter plunged into a deep, wooded valley. The pilot frantically flipped switches on the instrument panel. Joe prayed for the throbbing roar of the engine and rotors, but all he heard was the roar of the wind whistling past as they plummeted.

"Strap on your chutes!" Dodge hollered.

"What chute?" Joe shouted. "I don't usually carry one with me!"

Dodge pulled out four chutes, threw two of them to the Hardys and two up front to the trooper.

"Al!" Dodge yelled out. "Get this thing up as high as you can. We'll have to bail out!"

Dodge unlatched the door of a rear compartment and pulled out what looked to Frank to be orange parachutes. "Drift chutes," Dodge explained. "So they can find us."

Dodge crawled over to the Hardys and grabbed a cord with a hook on the end trailing out of Frank's chute.

"Hook this to that line up there," Dodge yelled, pointing at a wire line that sagged from the ceiling of the chopper. "It'll open your chute! After you jump, start counting. If you get to five and it isn't open, pull this." Dodge patted the emergency chute handle on Joe's chest.

"What if that doesn't open?" Joe asked.

"Start praying!"

Joe looked up front and saw the trooper unlocking Paul's handcuffs.

"Try to keep her steady till we can get out, Al!" Dodge yelled to the pilot. "Okay, let's go. Make sure to check your static line!"

His heart pounding, Joe watched the experienced crew hook their static lines on the sagging wire and then leap into empty space.

Suddenly Joe was at the head of the line. He hooked his static line, peered out at the mountains and trees, mustered every ounce of courage he had, and stepped out into the sky.

Buffeted by blasts of cold air, Joe sank through white puffs of cloud vapor. He was almost glad that he couldn't see the ground rushing toward him through the mist. He punched out the bottom of the cloud, and his parachute opened with a *woof* and a jerk on the harness that rattled his teeth. He spotted Frank a few hundred feet away, gliding down silently.

The trees came up fast, and Joe plunged right into the branches of a scraggly spruce. The chute snagged on a branch, yanking Joe to a halt with his feet dangling a few feet off the ground.

Frank landed in a clearing thirty yards away, rolling forward when he hit the ground. His chute caught a gust of wind and began to drag him, rocks banging into his back and shoulders. Frank slapped the harness release, and the chute blew free.

Frank found Joe bobbing in the tree, trying to untangle his parachute lines.

"Are you all right?" Frank asked his younger brother.

Joe smiled down at him. "Oh, I'm just hanging around. How about you?"

"My chute had a mind of its own, but I'm okay," Frank said.

Joe unhooked the harness, dropped to the ground, stumbled, and landed on his backside.

"The next time you want to get away from it all," Joe said as his brother helped him up, "I'm going to remind you of the peaceful week we spent in Alaska."

The chopper had crashed in a dense clump of trees at the far end of the clearing, about a half mile away. Dodge and Willis were roaming the area around the crash site when Frank and Joe ran up.

"Here they are!" Dodge said in his gruff voice. "Call everybody in, Willis."

Willis whistled twice, raised his hand high and made a circular motion, signaling the rest of the crew to come back.

"I was worried about you guys," Dodge said, striding over to the Hardys. "Thought you might've got strung up in the trees or something."

"I did," Joe said, "but it wasn't bad. I cut myself down. I had to leave the chute in the tree."

"That's okay," Dodge said. "We can always get more chutes."

The other two smoke jumpers, Rocky and Jim Carroll, ambled in.

Rocky's right arm hung stiffly at his side. "I got hung up on a branch," he said. "Nothing broken, but I think I yanked my arm out of the shoulder socket."

Dodge sighed. "This team hasn't had an injury in a hundred and fifty-three jumps—until today." He looked at Willis. "Who's missing?"

"Garcia, the trooper, and Al," Willis replied.

"Here comes the trooper now," Carroll said, pointing north across the clearing. "I don't see any sign of the prisoner."

"How convenient," Rocky muttered. "They arrest him for arson, and then the helicopter crashes. This is probably where he's going to start his next fire."

Frank didn't like Rocky's tone. "Maybe Paul's caught in a tree or something," he said.

"Did anybody see Al come down?" Dodge asked.

Frank heard a moan. It sounded as if it came from the helicopter, which had smashed into a thick clump of trees and was hanging forty-five feet off the ground. Frank heard the moan again.

"Up there!" Frank said. "It's coming from the chopper!"

Joe ran over and raised his eyes to the helicopter. He couldn't see anything through the window of the cockpit. He grabbed one of the lower branches of the nearest tree and started climbing.

"Hey, Joe, wait!" Dodge yelled. "Let one of us do that."

"I can do it," Joe called back, grunting as he pulled himself into a notch of the tree trunk.

Dodge shook his head, then gestured at Willis's parachute. "Start cutting your cords off," Dodge told him. "He's going to need a rope."

Willis cut the chute's canopy cords with his pocketknife.

"Get up on that branch above you," Dodge told Joe. "Then tie the rope around the trunk and loop it around yourself. That way you'll have a safety harness."

Another loud groan drifted out from the helicopter.

"Al?" Dodge yelled.

The moaning continued.

Dodge kicked the dirt. "He stayed with it all the way down! I told him to ditch."

Joe pulled himself out onto the branch that led to the cockpit. Then he gazed down at the group below him. "Okay, throw me the rope."

Willis threw the loop of cord up and Joe snatched it with one hand, holding on to the tree with his other hand. Then Joe propped his feet against a thick branch, leaned out, and unlatched the cockpit door.

Joe found Al lying on the floorboard, underneath the cockpit window. Al had a deep red gash across his temple, and he wasn't moving.

"Hey, Al," he said loudly. "Can you hear me?"

Al didn't respond.

"You're not going to make this easy for me, are you?" Joe muttered.

He let out some slack in his rope and climbed into the cockpit. The chopper shuddered and creaked. Joe crawled slowly over to the unconscious pilot.

Suddenly the nose dipped sharply and the helicopter lurched downward, metal scraping against the tree limbs. Joe froze and held his breath. The chopper swayed uneasily but didn't fall.

Joe untied his line and reached over to check Al, who was lying on his back. Joe patted him on the cheek a few times, but Al didn't move. Joe managed to grapple him to a sitting position. Maneuvering in the cramped space of the cockpit was hard, even with a small man like Al. Joe started to drag the pilot across the tilted floor toward the cockpit door, the chopper rocking restlessly.

"Joe, get out of there!" Frank yelled.

"Great idea!" Joe snapped. "What do you think I'm trying to do? Set up base camp?"

Joe inched a little closer to the door. The helicopter stirred fitfully now. "If I could just get out of here without actually moving," he muttered to himself.

Joe heard a long, low groan. He glanced at Al. The pilot was still out cold. Another lingering groan drifted into the cockpit. It wasn't Al. It wasn't anything human.

A sharp crack rang out like a gunshot. The helicopter lurched violently, and Joe knew what had happened. The weight of the helicopter had snapped the trunk of one of the trees. Joe was trapped inside as the giant metal cage plunged to the ground below.

Chapter

7

JOE HUGGED THE PILOT to the floor as the helicopter crashed through the branches. Metal screeched and huge tree limbs snapped like firecrackers. The chopper shuddered and bucked as it continued to plummet.

A violent jolt hurled Joe under the instrument panel. The nose heaved up, bashing Joe's back into the network of wires under the panel. The pilot's body slipped out of his grasp and tumbled toward the yawning doorway. Joe grabbed wildly at the pilot's leg and clutched his ankle.

The chopper tilted up wildly, throwing its occupants back against the seats. Joe wrapped his arms around the pilot in a bear hug, squeezed his eyes shut, and waited for the helicopter to smash into the ground with a final shattering impact.

The chopper swayed and groaned. After a dozen thundering heartbeats, Joe slowly opened his eyes and peered out the open door. The ground was still a good twenty feet away, but the helicopter didn't seem to be in any hurry to get there.

"Joe!" Frank called out. "Are you all right?"

"You tell me!" Joe shouted back. "What's holding this thing up?"

Frank eyed the wreckage in the dense clump of trees and sucked in his breath. The chopper was almost standing on end, pointing skyward. The nose was halfway up a tall birch tree. The only thing holding it up was a bent rotor blade tangled in the thick branches of another tree— and the twisted blade looked as if it might snap any second.

"We'd better get them out of there fast," Dodge said.

Frank nodded. "Joe! Can you move the pilot?"

Joe glanced down at the unconscious man. A low moan drifted from the pilot's lips, and his eyes fluttered open. "What hit me?" he groaned, touching a large purplish bruise on his forehead.

"Just about everything," Joe replied. "The controls, the floor, the seat—if you had a kitchen sink in here it would have whacked you, too. The landing was a little rough."

"Are we down?"

"Not yet. Do you think you can sit up?"

The pilot nodded weakly, and Joe helped him up.

"I think Al's okay," Joe shouted down to his brother. "But we're going to need a little help getting out of here."

Frank glanced around, and his eyes landed on one of the discarded parachutes. "That's just what we need." He looked at the smoke jumpers. "If we each grab an end of that chute—"

"Right," Dodge said. "We can use it as a net."

Joe peered down at the makeshift safety net spread out below the cockpit. "Are you sure that thing is strong enough?"

"Do you have any better ideas?" Frank countered.

"I don't know," Joe responded.

The chopper rocked and creaked.

"You hang around and think about it," the pilot said, crawling to the doorway. "I'm out of here."

Joe watched him tumble out of the cockpit and plop down into the middle of the open parachute. Frank and the smoke jumpers gently lowered the chute to the ground, and Rocky and Willis carried the pilot safely away from the dangling helicopter.

"Okay, Joe," Frank said when the two men came back and took up their ends of the jerry-rigged net. "Now it's your turn."

Joe sighed, took a deep breath, and forced himself to step out the door. He wanted to yell something like "Geronimo!" but what came out was more like "Geraggh!" He thought free-fall was supposed to be fun, but he was having a hard time getting into it. He hit the billowing silk with arms and legs flailing. His only injury was a slightly bruised ego.

Dodge knelt down and examined Al's head. There was an ugly bruise across his forehead and a bloody gash in his temple.

"Did anybody grab the first aid kit?" Dodge asked.

"It's still in the chopper," Willis said.

"Terrific," Dodge muttered.

Frank was studying the precariously perched wreck. "It wouldn't take much to bring her down. Throw a line around the landing gear, give it a few good tugs, and get out of the way."

"Sounds like a good idea," Dodge said. "Let's do it."

Rocky used his good arm to toss Dodge his chute. "Here you go, Homer, use mine."

Frank pulled out his pocketknife and helped Dodge cut cords to make a rope.

"Everyone grab hold," Dodge said after he threw the line over the landing gear and grabbed both ends of it. "As soon as that useless hunk of metal starts to come down, everybody clear. I don't want any more injuries. Understood?"

"Understood," Willis said.

"Here we go," Dodge said. "One, two, three, pull!"

The helicopter shifted and slipped a few feet.

"One more pull should do it," Dodge said. "Ready? Pull!"

The chopper tottered and started to fall.

"Run!" Dodge yelled.

Everybody scattered as the metal bird smashed into the ground in a crumpled heap of twisted metal and shattered glass.

Willis crawled into the wreck and out with the first aid kit and an emergency flare gun.

Dodge cleaned the pilot's wound and wrapped a bandage around his head. Halfway through the operation, Al passed out.

"I think he may have a concussion," Dodge told the others. "How's everybody else?"

"No serious injuries," Willis reported. "Garcia is still missing."

"I hope Garcia stays missing," Rocky grumbled. "Leave him to the wolves and the bears. It would serve him right for putting us through all this misery."

Frank was getting tired of Rocky's attitude. "You aren't blaming Paul for the crash, are you?" he demanded. "He couldn't have done anything to sabotage the helicopter. He was handcuffed and guarded the whole flight."

"And he could have been killed when the chopper went down," Joe added.

"That may be," Rocky said, "but we wouldn't be out here if it weren't for him. We wouldn't have had to make the jump at Wonder Lake, so we wouldn't have had to make this trip back."

"Furthermore," Dodge pitched in, "if he's innocent, why'd he take off? It never helps your case when you run."

Trooper Haynes, sitting on a rock behind the outstretched pilot, stood up. "Forget about Garcia. We've got a much bigger problem right now, which is how we get rescued."

"They'll find us," Dodge said. "I heard Al on the radio while everybody was jumping. He gave our position as ten miles west of Nenana. I figure we're about an hour from Fairbanks."

"In a car maybe," the trooper said. "But you know this country better than I do. We're in the middle of nowhere. How are they going to find us?"

"Good question," Dodge said. He stroked his thick walrus mustache. "I've got an idea. How many chutes do we have, Willis?"

"Four," Willis answered.

"Bring them here," Dodge instructed. "I'll take them to that rocky clearing over there and make an arrow with them that can be spotted from the air."

"I'll help," Willis offered.

"I can do it myself," Dodge said. "You take everyone and start a search for Garcia. Fan out in a circle. It's possible that the guy might've gotten hurt I don't think we'll find him, but we should at least make the effort."

"You're right, Homer," Frank said, pleased

that Dodge showed some concern for Paul's safety.

"If I see a search plane or chopper, I'll fire the flare gun to get its attention," Dodge said. "Then I'll fire two shots, which means everybody should head back here."

Frank and Joe headed downhill, weaving through a maze of pine and spruce trees.

"Why would Paul run?" Joe wondered out loud as they threaded their way into a narrow ravine with few trees.

"We don't know he ran," Frank responded. "Maybe the wind carried him farther than anybody else. Maybe he's trying to find us right now. Maybe a bear got him."

Joe's eyes widened. "Do you really think a bear might have gotten him?"

"Not really," Frank admitted. "I also don't believe he started those forest fires."

Frank froze in his tracks and held up his hand, signaling Joe to stop.

"What is it?" Joe asked.

Frank raised his index finger to his lips and then pointed to a rustling bush about twenty feet away.

Joe didn't know what was in there—but from the way the bush was shaking, he figured it was something *big*.

Suddenly a brown wall of fur rose up behind the bush. Deep-set black eyes focused on the

Hardys. A ferocious roar howled out of a mouth bristling with huge, sharp teeth.

"Uh," Joe croaked in a harsh whisper, gulping hard. "Do you remember what Paul said to do if a grizzly—"

The huge bear exploded out of the bush and barreled across the ravine in a growling blur.

As the bear hurtled toward them, Frank's mind latched on to one thing Paul had told them—you can't outrun a grizzly. It's no use even trying.

Chapter

8

JOE COULD THINK of only one thing to do when staring into the face of a charging grizzly.

"Run!" he screamed.

The bear thundered along the small ravine, flattening a small bush in its path and roaring a deadly challenge. The creature was as big as a car—and almost as fast.

Frank's mind raced, one step ahead of the blind panic that threatened to overcome him. He knew they had only one chance. "No!" he yelled, grabbing his brother's arm before Joe could bolt.

"Get down!" Frank shouted, dropping to his knees and jerking Joe down with him. Then he ducked his head down to the ground and covered his head with his hands.

Joe stared in disbelief. Frank was giving up,

curling up and waiting to be eaten alive. "Are you crazy?" he bellowed, shaking his brother's shoulder. "We're sitting ducks!"

"Get your head down!" Frank snapped in an urgent whisper. "Don't move, don't talk, don't make any noise. Don't even breathe out loud!"

Frank's tone gave Joe a little hope that his brother actually knew what he was doing. Besides, he didn't really have a choice now. The raging bear was almost on top of him.

Joe hunched over, his knees to his chest, his face buried in the rough grass. He wasn't worried about breathing too loud. Joe had no intention of breathing until this was over—and maybe not even then, he told himself grimly. If Frank's plan—whatever it was—didn't work, they wouldn't have to worry about breathing anymore.

The grizzly's angry roar faded to a low growl. Joe knew the animal was close—*very* close. He could feel the bear's hot breath on the back of his neck. It took every ounce of willpower to remain absolutely still.

The growl shifted to a loud snuffling. Something cold and wet brushed Joe's hand. He could smell the musty odor of the bear's fur and knew the bear was smelling him, too. The grizzly's nose was working overtime, prodding Joe's hand, sniffing around his clothes.

After the longest thirty seconds in Joe's life, the bear lost interest in him and shuffled off. Joe peeked out and saw the big grizzly nosing around

Frank. Apparently satisfied that Frank wasn't a threat or a tasty treat, the bear started to lumber off.

Then the bear glanced back at Joe. Joe tucked his head back down and did his best imitation of a dull, boring rock. He didn't budge until he heard the grizzly crashing through the underbrush in the distance.

A loud *boom* echoed down the valley as Joe got up off the ground. "Was that the flare gun?" he asked.

Frank brushed himself off and scanned the sky. "I don't know. I don't see a flare."

Two shots rang out, one right after the other.

"That's Homer's signal to head back," Joe confirmed.

The Hardys moved out cautiously, watching for the bear at every step and hoping it was long gone.

"How did you know what to do when the bear attacked?" Joe asked.

"I remembered what Paul told us," Frank replied.

Joe frowned. "I thought he said you were supposed to wave your hands and talk in a loud voice."

"That's what you do *before* the bear charges," Frank responded. "If the bear comes after you, it's a whole different ball game."

"I'm glad you remembered the rules," Joe said.

"And I'm glad you listened to Paul more carefully than I did."

"It wasn't just Paul. I also picked this up at the lodge." Frank reached into his back pocket and pulled out a folded brochure. " 'If the bear approaches, do not try to run away,' " he read. " 'If contact is imminent, fall to the ground, tuck into a fetal position, and play dead.' "

"I still can't believe the bear was dumb enough to fall for that trick," Joe said.

Frank grinned. "Just be glad the grizzly wasn't smart enough to read the brochure."

The Hardys climbed uphill, anxious to rejoin the smoke jumpers. They pushed through a thicket of mulberry and crowberry bushes so dense and high that they couldn't see more than a few yards ahead.

As they moved higher and the slope grew steeper, the bushes thinned out and gave way to a rocky terrain. Frank's legs started to ache, and a raw blister nagged his right heel. The Hardys groped for the branches of bushes struggling to grow in the flaky schist, pulling themselves slowly upward.

"It was a lot easier going down," Joe huffed. "My legs feel like lead weights."

As they neared the top of the rise, Frank spotted a plume of smoke rising into the blue sky. When they reached the summit, he saw the source of the smoke. The wreck of the helicopter was engulfed in a ball of fire, and the flames were spreading to the nearby trees.

Joe gaped. "What happened? That fire's so intense, I can feel the heat from here!"

The Hardys ran over to where Dodge crouched next to the injured pilot, in the shade of a large boulder a good, safe distance from the fire. The two other smoke jumpers and the state trooper stood nearby, watching the blaze.

"Shouldn't we do something about the chopper?" Joe asked anxiously. "It could burn down the whole forest!"

"We can control it," Dodge said grimly. "The wind's blowing south, and fire burns slowly downhill. The good news is, the flames will draw attention to this area. That means we'll get rescued sooner."

Frank watched the fire leap from the chopper to the surrounding trees, turning them into blazing torches. The smoke billowed high in the sky, blotting out the sun. Frank wiped his forehead. Even here, the heat was hard to take.

"We need to dig a fire line around the chopper now," Dodge said as he stood up. "That's why I called everybody back. Good thing Willis got all the packs out of the chopper before it exploded."

Joe heard a crack and a loud popping noise. He glanced in the direction of the sound and couldn't believe what his eyes verified—a mound of rocks consumed by fire exploded into jagged fragments.

"Let's get moving," Dodge said. "Willis, take Frank and Joe and start digging."

"I've still got one good arm," Rocky protested. "You don't have to send a kid to do my job."

"Frank and Joe aren't kids," Dodge said, "and they both have *two* good arms.

"And don't you say anything, either," Dodge added, turning to Carroll. "I saw the way you were hobbling around. You've got a bad sprain, maybe even a broken ankle. You're just too stubborn to admit it."

Willis looked at the Hardys. "Let's get the packs. I left them over there behind that rock."

Joe cast a troubled glance at the growing blaze. "What happens if the fire line doesn't hold?"

Willis shrugged. "It happens all the time. There's not a whole lot you can do when a fire does jump the line except back off and get out of the way."

"What if you can't get out of the way?" Joe responded in a worried tone.

Willis nodded past the burning wreck. "Ask the trees."

Joe turned and saw flames swirling in the trees, leaping from branch to branch. He couldn't imagine how a few guys with shovels could stop the fiery demon.

The Hardys followed Willis to the spot behind the rock where he had left the packs.

"Let's see," Willis said. "Joe, you take Carroll's pack, and Frank can take Rocky's gear."

"You've got a few rations and extra clothes in here," Willis explained as he handed them the packs. "There's also an aluminized pup tent."

"What's that for?" Joe asked.

"It's for when you've got no other choice," Willis told him. "The tent's fireproof, up to about eight hundred degrees. If you're surrounded by flames and there's no way out, you wrap yourself in that."

"And you'll survive?" Frank asked in amazement.

"For about ten or fifteen minutes," Willis said grimly. "But it's no fun, kid. Think of a baked potato."

Willis patted a tool hooked on a strap on the side of one of the packs. Joe thought it looked like a cross between an axe and a hoe. "This is a Pulaski," he said. "No smoke jumper goes to work without one."

Frank slung the pack over his shoulder. "Okay, let's go fight a fire."

Willis gazed at the ground and frowned. "Hold on a second." He walked around the rock and came back scratching his head. "Hey, Homer!" he called out. "Did you take one of the packs?"

"What do you mean?" Dodge yelled back. "Aren't they all there?"

Willis trudged back toward Dodge, and the Hardys went with him. "We only have three packs," Willis said. "We had four a little while ago."

"Are you sure you got all four packs out of the chopper?" Dodge responded.

"Positive," Willis said. "It took me a while to find all four, but I did it."

Dodge stroked his mustache. "Well, the pack didn't just get up and walk away by itself."

"Maybe it had a little help," Rocky suggested. "It's not too hard to figure out. One pack is missing, right? What else is gone?"

"My prisoner," the state trooper answered.

Rocky nodded. "Put those two facts together and what do you get?"

Dodge gazed silently at the blackened hulk of the blazing wreck. "You get an arsonist on the run."

Chapter

9

"THIS DOESN'T LOOK GOOD for Paul," Frank said as the Hardys followed Willis toward the burning helicopter.

"Why is it any worse now than it was before?" Joe replied. "He's already been arrested for arson."

"Think about it," Frank said. "The helicopter crashes, and Paul takes off. Then he sneaks back and steals a fire fighter's pack."

Joe nodded. "And then the chopper goes up in flames, starting another forest fire."

Frank checked the black smoke uncoiling from the burning wreck. Paul had told them that he had charted all the fires on a map, and he had admitted that he was near the source of the fire every time. If he really was an arsonist, why would he have mentioned the map?

71

"This is where we'll start the fire line," Willis shouted to be heard over the fire. The smoke jumper scraped off two or three inches of topsoil with his Pulaski. "You dig the line with the hoe, and chop trees, shrubs, and roots with the axe."

Trying to ignore the heat, Joe got down on his knees and began scraping with the hoe side of the tool. This had definitely become a working vacation, he thought ruefully.

A few hours later Joe made a mental note to cross "smoke jumper" off his list of career choices. It was hot, hard work. He was about to take a break when he heard a faint, buzzing sound. He looked up and saw a single-engine plane circling the rocks where Dodge had made the giant arrow out of parachutes.

"It's a spotter plane!" Willis yelled, pointing to the sky. "They've found us!"

Joe dropped his Pulaski. "How's it going to land here?"

"It's not," Willis answered. "The pilot will radio back to our base and they'll send another chopper for us."

After circling the area a few more times the small plane left.

"Okay, guys, help is on the way," Willis called out. "In the meantime, let's make some line."

Working with renewed energy, Frank, Joe, and Willis managed to complete the fire line before they were picked up an hour later.

*   *   *

On their way to Fairbanks once again, the Hardys watched emergency medics attend to Al Brunner, who lay stretched out on the floor.

Frank overheard Carroll talking to Willis about "that stuff with Dodge and the reprimand," but the roar of the engine drowned out their conversation. Then Frank heard Dodge talking to the pilot of the rescue chopper.

"For all we know, he's out starting more fires," Dodge said.

A few minutes later Dodge came back and sat down on the bench next to Frank and Joe. Frank decided to talk to the smoke jumper about Paul.

"Paul plotted all the fires in the park this summer on a map," Frank told Homer Dodge. "Every one of them happened near one of his treks. Why would he keep incriminating evidence like that, and why would he tell us about it?"

Dodge stared at Frank. Then he shook his head. "Arsonists can be pretty crafty. Maybe he thought telling you about the map would give him an alibi. If he told you about it, then you wouldn't suspect him of starting the fires."

Joe leaned forward. "Would *you* do something like that if you were the one setting the fires?"

Dodge stroked his mustache. "Probably not," he admitted. "But let me ask you something. If Garcia's not the arsonist, why did he run?"

73

THE HARDY BOYS CASEFILES

"Good question," Joe admitted. "I don't have an answer for it."

"But we plan to find one," Frank said resolutely.

The helicopter landed at Fort Wainwright in Fairbanks shortly after nine o'clock that night. Dodge's crew had been up for two days, fought two forest fires, and survived a helicopter crash. An ambulance met them at the runway and took Brunner, Rocky, and Carroll to the hospital.

"Are you two going to stick with us or head back to the park?" Dodge asked after the ambulance drove off. "I wouldn't blame you for moving on after everything that's happened."

"We've gone through a lot to get here," Frank said. "Do you have a place we can stay tonight?"

"Sure," Dodge said. "You can bunk with us in the dorm. Then if you want, you can take the train back to the park tomorrow morning."

"Thanks, Homer," Frank said.

A van pulled up to take the smoke jumpers to their dorm. As he climbed into the van, Frank saw a blue car pull up beside the plane. The car had a state trooper emblem on the door. Two men got out of the car, one wearing a suit and the other a trooper's uniform.

"Those must be Trooper Haynes's bosses," Frank said to Joe.

As the two men walked over to Haynes and

Dodge, Frank unlatched the van window so he could hear what they said.

"We don't know quite what happened. Something went wrong with our fuel line," Dodge said to the man in the suit.

"I had to take off Garcia's handcuffs when we bailed out," Haynes explained, "and then he got away from us after the crash."

"We still have a spotter plane out looking for him," the man in uniform said.

"Give me time to clean up, and I'll get back out there," Haynes said. "That torcher is mine!"

The smoke jumpers' dorm was a two-story building about a mile from the landing field. Inside, the Hardys found offices, a weight room, and a lounge on the first floor.

"Wow," Joe said when Willis showed them the lounge. "You've got everything here: a pool table, jukebox, video games, even a big screen TV."

"And there's a fully stocked kitchen over there," Willis said, nodding to the far side of the big room.

There was one man in the lounge, shooting pool by himself. Willis introduced the Hardys to Buck Stevens, a twenty-eight-year-old plumber from Silver Spring, Maryland. Then Willis left to find bedding for the brothers.

Joe gave Buck a quick summary of the helicopter crash and what happened afterward.

"Sounds worse than a 115-pound packout," Buck said, knocking the nine ball in a corner pocket.

"What's that?" Joe asked.

"The final test of rookie camp," Buck replied. "You hike three and a half miles through the mountains with a 115-pound pack, and if you don't get back before three and a half hours, they make you do it again." Buck sank the three ball on a bank shot. "But after what you guys have been through, it sounds like a packout would be a breeze for you."

Joe noticed a sign on the wall above the pool table: It only hurts until the pain goes away.

A little while later Carroll limped in with an elastic support bandage wrapped around his ankle.

"So," Carroll said, scanning the refrigerator, "have we scared you guys out of becoming smoke jumpers?"

"I don't know," Joe replied. "Eating smoke and digging fire line is starting to get in my blood."

"It can do that to you," Carroll said, pulling the tab top on a diet cola and closing the refrigerator door. He nodded at the other smoke jumper, who put up his cue stick and left the lounge. "You spend all summer doing this kind of work and it makes what you do the rest of the year look tame."

"What do you do the rest of the year?" Frank asked.

"I teach high school science in Yakima, Washington," Carroll answered. "I'm not the only teacher on the base, either. We have a few college profs, plus a lot of college students. The summer months are high fire season, so the BLM takes on plenty of extra workers."

"Do you like working with Homer?" Frank asked.

"Oh sure, Homer's a great guy," Carroll replied. "He'll get you in and out of a fire without anybody getting hurt, and that's quite a feat. It's too bad he has to quit. I can't imagine him sitting behind a desk."

Frank remembered something. "By the way, I couldn't help but hear something you said to Willis on the helicopter," Frank said. "You were talking about Homer and some kind of reprimand?"

Just then Dodge walked in. Carroll looked at the Hardys. "Why don't I give you guys a quick tour?" he suggested.

Frank glanced at Joe. "Go on, I'll catch up with you later," Frank said. "I want to talk to Homer."

As Joe and Carroll left, Dodge poured himself a cup of coffee.

"Homer, are the state troopers searching for Paul?" Frank asked.

Dodge nodded. "They've stopped for the night, though," he said, blowing on his coffee. "I don't think they're going to find him. This is big country, and Garcia knows how to survive in the wilderness. I'm afraid we may have to fight a few more fires before he's caught."

"I know it's hard to believe after everything that's happened, but do you think somebody else might have planted that evidence in Paul's truck?" Frank asked. "Is it possible that Paul's being framed?"

Dodge sipped his coffee, then stared at Frank. "Who'd frame him?" he asked, peering over the rim of his cup.

Frank shrugged. "I don't know."

Frank noticed a photograph of Dodge on the wall. He was wearing hunting gear and standing with a few other hunters next to a dead caribou. One of the men had a beard, and Frank was sure he'd seen him somewhere before. He just couldn't place the face.

"Who are those guys?" Frank asked, pointing.

"Me and some of my hunting buddies from long ago," Dodge said. "I don't hunt anymore, though. It was starting to wear me out."

"Who's that on the end, the guy with the beard?"

Dodge paused a few seconds before answering. "That, my friend, is the fellow you saw arguing with Al Brunner yesterday—none other than the T-shirt king himself, Jeff Rankin."

Frank was suddenly intrigued by the photo. "Did you and Rankin do a lot of hunting together?"

Dodge sipped his coffee. "Like I said, it was a long time ago."

Frank walked over to the photo. "That's a weird gun Rankin's holding," Frank noted. "I've never seen one like it."

Dodge stepped over beside Frank. "It's an over-under," Dodge said. "A Weatherby forty-four, I think. It has a twelve-gauge double-barrel on top and a twenty-two caliber barrel on the bottom."

Frank studied the photo and Rankin's shotgun, recalling the .22 bullet in Paul's tire. If Rose hadn't shot at them, maybe Rankin had.

Dodge took another sip of coffee. "You're probably bushed. I know I am. Come on, I'll show you your room. Then I'm going to conk out."

Frank sat on the edge of his bed for a few minutes. Joe was still off with Carroll, and Frank was too wired to sleep. Thoughts kept swirling in his head. Frank wondered again what kind of reprimand Carroll had been talking about with Willis. He wondered, too, how Jeff Rankin felt about Homer Dodge now, and whether the two men's friendship had anything to do with the fires.

The thoughts didn't add up to anything, though. Frank got up and decided to go shoot some pool.

Downstairs, Frank passed an office door with Dodge's name on it. The door was open, and the office was empty. Frank couldn't resist the temptation to try to find the answers to some of his questions. He stepped into the office, shut the door, and flicked on the desk lamp, though he still wasn't sure what he wanted to find.

Alone in the office, Frank turned to the file cabinets on the wall behind the desk. He tried to open the file cabinet on the end. It was locked.

Frank had been on too many cases to be stopped by a lock. He slipped a lock-pick out of his wallet and deftly worked the cabinet open.

Quickly Frank started leafing through the file folders. They appeared to be personnel records for the smoke jumpers. Frank noticed that Willis's file was much thicker than the others. He pulled it out.

Besides the usual personal data sheets, the file contained a sheaf of documents dating from eight years earlier. The papers were full of technical lingo Frank couldn't understand, but he got the general idea. Willis had received an official reprimand eight years earlier for deliberately starting fires to train new jumpers.

Frank froze when he heard footsteps moving down the hall. He slipped the file in place and quietly shut the drawer.

The footsteps drew closer. Frank scanned the office for another way out, but there was only the one door.

Frank turned to it as it flew open. Willis stood there, his huge form filling the doorway. When his gaze fell on Frank, his face was red with rage.

Chapter

10

"WHAT ARE YOU DOING in here?" Willis demanded harshly.

Frank thought of a number of excuses, none of them believable. Frank wasn't about to ask Willis if someone who started forest fires to train people might also start them for fun.

"I was—ah—looking for some applications," Frank finally responded. "Homer told me they were in here." Homer hadn't told him anything like that, but Willis wouldn't know that. Frank could tell he didn't totally buy his story, though. "Do you know where they are?"

Willis went to Dodge's desk, opened one of the lower drawers, and pulled out two applications.

Frank pretended to read one of them, but he did it mainly to avoid Willis's icy glare.

Willis stared at Frank for a few more seconds. Then he yawned. Frank inwardly breathed a sigh of relief.

"Let's go to the lounge," Willis said, turning out the light in Dodge's office. "I'll make you one of my knockout specials."

"What's that?" Frank asked.

"Two aspirin in a root beer float," Willis said.

In the lounge Willis and Frank found Carroll and Joe, back from their tour, sitting at the table, eating sandwiches. "Hey, Willis," Carroll said, "I was just telling Joe what Homer always says about being a smoke jumper. Remember? 'What makes you a smoke jumper is not jumping out of an airplane, but—' "

" 'Eating smoke and digging fire lines,' " Willis completed the sentence with a smile. "Repeat after me!" Willis added, imitating Homer's gruff voice. Carroll joined him on the chant. "You are not a skydiver! You are not a parachutist! You are a fire fighter!"

Watching the performance, Frank wondered if one of the fire fighters was also a fire starter.

Frank and Joe's room had two bunks and a chest, a closet with sliding doors, and a sink with a mirror above it. Tarpaper had been taped over the window to block out the midnight sun so they could sleep.

Early the next morning Frank untacked a corner of the tarpaper to peer outside. A bright ray of sun streaked across Joe's pillow, making him squint and roll over.

"Get up," Frank said. "We're burning daylight."

Joe groaned and pulled the covers up. "Who cares? There's plenty of it to burn up here."

Frank jabbed his brother in the shoulder. "But there's only one train back to Denali today."

A few minutes later Frank stood under the shower nozzle and gloried in the simple pleasure of hot, steaming water. While he let the spray work out the kinks in his muscles, he pondered what had happened over the past days. The fire at Wonder Lake, the gunshot that ran them off the road, the incident at the Sure Shot, the helicopter crash—all of these incidents raised questions that Frank still couldn't answer.

Was Rose Hudiburg so bitter about breaking up with Paul that she would try to kill him? Why was Jeff Rankin nosing around the chopper yesterday? And what about Willis? Frank wondered if Willis knew anything about explosives and timers.

What Frank found most perplexing, though, was the strange behavior of Paul Garcia. Why did he run from the helicopter crash? Or *did* he run? If he didn't, what happened to the other smoke jumper's pack? And where was Paul now?

Coming back from the shower, Frank found Joe reading a sign taped to the sliding door of the closet. The sign listed the ten standard fire-fighting orders. When Frank walked up, Joe pointed to number four—Always have an escape plan.

"I guess Paul had a plan," Joe said.

Frank didn't answer.

Joe turned to his brother. "Is something bothering you?"

Frank shrugged. "I found out something interesting last night while Carroll was showing you around." Frank told Joe about Willis's reprimand eight years earlier.

"A fire fighter starting forest fires," Joe said, shaking his head. "That's pretty sick."

"It makes a certain amount of sense, though," Frank said. "What would be the ideal training for a smoke jumper?"

Joe nodded. "Fighting real fires."

"And think about this," Frank said. "A smoke jumper is the first on the scene at a fire. He would be able to cover up any evidence of arson. He could literally bury it."

Joe frowned. "I don't get it. So Willis started a few small fires a long time ago to train smoke jumpers. What's his motive now?"

Frank shrugged. "Maybe Willis is working for Rankin. A successful entrepreneur like Rankin could afford to pay a smoke jumper to do his dirty work for him. Maybe Willis decided that if he's going to live dangerously, he might as well make it pay."

"I think you're wrong," Joe said. "It seems to

me that smoke jumpers would do this kind of work even if they didn't get paid at all."

There was a knock on the door, and Dodge poked his head inside.

"Just the men I wanted to see," Dodge said. Willis came in behind him. "I've got a proposition for you guys."

"Name it," Frank said.

"Willis and I are taking a crew out on a practice jump this morning," Dodge said. "I thought you two might want to come along."

"We were going to catch the train back to Denali," Frank said.

Dodge looked at his watch. "You can still do that. It leaves in about an hour and a half."

"I told Homer you guys wouldn't want to go," Willis spoke up. "I told him you probably got a big enough taste of a smoke jumper's life yesterday."

"Maybe you should have talked *to* us before you decided to talk *for* us," Frank answered.

"Well, I'm asking you now," Dodge said. "This time you'll get to jump from a few thousand feet instead of a few hundred. How about it?"

Frank and Joe checked with each other.

"I'll tell you what," Dodge added. "Trooper Haynes is flying back to Healy this afternoon. I'll see if I can get you guys a ride with him. The plane's a twin-engine six-seater, so there should be room. Think it over. I'll go talk to Haynes."

After Homer and Willis left, Frank looked at

his brother. "Why don't you go on the jump?" Frank suggested. "See if you can find out more about Willis."

"Okay," Joe said. "What are you going to do?"

"I'll take the train back," Frank said. "It doesn't make sense for both of us to hang around here all day when most of the evidence is back at Denali. You can fly back later with Haynes."

"What will you do when you get back to the park?"

"I'll rent a car and drive out to Paul's cabin," Frank said. "I want to see that map. Maybe it will tell us something."

"What should I do when I get back?"

"See what you can find out about Jeff Rankin. I'll meet you back at the lodge."

There was another knock and Dodge stepped in. "All set, if you guys want to go," he told them.

"I do," Joe said. "Frank's taking the train back."

Frank gave Dodge a sheepish grin. "I can wait a while before I go skydiving again, Homer," he said. "Please don't take it personally."

"I won't," Dodge said, shaking hands with Frank. "You take care of yourself." Then Dodge turned to Joe. "Let's go. The crew's already on the plane."

"What about breakfast?" Joe said.

"You don't want to eat before a jump, Joe,"

Dodge said. "You might lose it. We'll be jumping at a spot here at the base. Afterward is the best time to eat."

The DC-3 flew for about half an hour before it reached the jump site. Then it circled three times just as it would at a fire.

Willis was the spotter, lying on the floor beside the open door, wearing headphones so he could talk with the pilot, Ken Stover.

Stover told Willis he would jump the crew at two thousand feet. Dodge lay on the right side of the door, mainly so he could watch the jumps.

Joe and the other crew members sat straddle-legged on the floor, each man fitting snugly between the legs of the man behind him so all sixteen jumpers and their equipment would fit in the plane. Joe was relieved to know that so many others would be jumping with him.

On the first pass Willis dropped the orange drift chutes. On the next he estimated the distance and direction the wind had blown the chutes, so he could tell how far ahead of their target he should drop the jumpers.

The sixteen jumpers were divided into groups of four, with one group jumping on each run over the landing arca. Joc's group went first.

They stood in front of the open door, one behind the other, the front man with his left foot forward. Joe stood behind Carroll, his right foot forward. That way, after Carroll jumped, Joe could take one step forward and be in the lead jumper's position.

Willis stood up and nudged Joe on the shoulder. "Hand me your static line," Willis yelled.

Joe handed Willis his line, which had a hook on the end. Dodge stood up and put his arm around Joe. "Just remember to count to five!" he shouted in Joe's ear.

The plane banked and leveled off. Wind and empty air roared on the other side of the wide open hatchway. Joe watched Willis tap the jumper in front on the calf of his left leg. The jumper disappeared.

Then it was Joe's turn. He had jumped the day before, but Joe still felt nervous—terrified, actually. He recalled the time he and Frank had gone to an amusement park that had a roller coaster called the Death Ride. All he could think about the week before was going on the Death Ride—but when they got there, Joe panicked. If Frank hadn't called him a sissy, Joe would never have gone on it.

In the DC-3 Joe felt the same way—this jump could very well become his own death ride. Joe felt as if he were stepping onto the trapdoor at his own hanging. Then he felt the tap on his left leg.

Joe stepped with his left foot, so the wind drift wouldn't throw him face first into the plane's tail to his left.

The rush of fear hit him like his worst nightmare. Joe had never been so shocked. He felt as if he were tumbling into a deep black hole.

Joe started counting. One thousand one, one thousand two, one thousand three, one thousand four . . . They were the longest seconds in Joe's life.

He couldn't wait to get to one thousand five, but when he did, nothing happened! Joe waited a few more seconds, desperately hoping he had counted too fast, and the chute would pop open. There was no comforting tug on the harness, no reassuring flutter of silk.

Joe plummeted out of control, arms and legs flailing wildly. He couldn't make himself fly—and that was the only thing that would save him from being smashed to a bloody pulp when he hit the ground.

Chapter

11

JOE JERKED HIS HEAD around and saw his static line trailing out of his main chute. He thrashed at the sky for a few seconds, his legs pumping futilely as he hurtled downward.

He wanted to scream, but nothing came out of his mouth. Or maybe it did, and Joe just couldn't hear it because of the rush of the wind.

Then Joe came to his senses and remembered the emergency chute on his chest. He yanked the handle. Fabric billowed out. Then the chute grabbed him and jerked him backward. Joe almost did a back flip, his feet swinging up.

The emergency parachute wasn't as big as the main chute, so it didn't catch as much air. Joe's feet hit the ground hard, sending a shock wave up his legs. Joe barely noticed. He was just glad to be alive and on the ground.

The plane landed a few minutes later, and Joe rushed over as Willis climbed out.

"Willis!" Joe yelled, only inches from the man's face. "Something happened to my static line! My chute didn't open."

Willis was stunned. "I can't believe it, Joe. I hooked your static line myself."

"Yeah, I saw you do it," Joe responded sharply. "Maybe someone else should've hooked it."

Joe spun around and stomped off. He was so mad he could barely think. His heart was still pounding in his ears. The terror of the almost fatal fall was behind him, but his body was still on red alert.

Willis ran after him. "Joe, I'm really sorry," he pleaded. "I don't know wha—"

"Forget it," Joe snapped.

Dodge came running up. "What's going on?"

Joe cast a glance at Willis.

"Something happened to Joe's static line," Willis said nervously. "I hooked it up myself."

Joe walked toward his chute, lying in the grass between the runways. He could hear Dodge ripping into Willis as he gathered up the silk. "Be in the superintendent's office in half an hour!" Dodge bellowed.

Dodge walked out to Joe, who was rolling up his chute. "Joe, I am very sorry."

Joe didn't respond. He just kept gathering the silk into a big ball.

Homer scratched his head, then patted Joe on the back. "I guess you learned the hard way what every smoke jumper learns sooner or later," Dodge said, "the only way you can be sure is to hook that static line yourself."

Dodge kept talking to Joe as they walked back to the barracks, but Joe didn't hear him. All Joe could think about was that one small piece of metal—the emergency handle—had saved him from plunging to his death.

"It sounds like someone wanted you out of the way permanently," Frank said after Joe told him the story that afternoon in the lobby of the Eagle's Nest Lodge.

"Maybe," Joe said, putting his feet up on the big oak coffee table in front of the couch. Joe had just arrived on a shuttle bus from Healy, where the trooper's plane had landed about a half hour earlier. "But now that I've had a few hours to think about it, it could've been just an accident."

"Did you find out about Willis and the reprimand?" Frank asked.

"Jim Carroll told me that both fires Willis had set were in areas that had burned the year before. It was a wet summer, and the crew didn't have much to do. Willis just wanted to keep the jumpers from losing their edge. What Willis didn't plan on was the wind changing. One of the fires spread outside the burned area, though it didn't go far."

Frank stroked his chin, trying to decide what to think about Willis. "We shouldn't rule him out as a suspect. When he found me in Homer's office yesterday, he seemed suspicious. Maybe he thinks you and I are onto him."

Joe sat up. "Who are our other suspects?"

"The most obvious one is Paul," Frank replied. "And then there's Rankin, because he was nosing around the helicopter before we left. I can't help but think that he had something to do with the crash."

"What about Rose?" Joe asked.

"Cross her off the list," Frank replied. "I found out she was giving a lecture at the Denali Park Hotel the night somebody took a shot at us. She stayed after the lecture to talk with some German tourists. According to the desk clerk, she didn't leave the hotel until after midnight."

"She probably really does use that gun in her purse to scare away bears," Frank added.

"So what do we do now?" Joe asked.

"I'm going to rent a car and drive out to Paul's cabin to see his map," Frank said. "I haven't made it there yet. If I can get into his cabin and find the map, it might tell us something to help crack the case."

Joe was mildly surprised. "So you really think Paul was framed?"

"He didn't have any reason to start those forest fires," Frank pointed out.

"And Rankin did?"

"It's possible," Frank said. "Rankin could have wanted to get revenge for losing the concession deal. I know it sounds warped, but someone who would start a forest fire has to be a little unbalanced. That's why you need to go out to Rankin's house this afternoon. See if you can find any evidence that might tie him to the arson incidents."

"And also any proof that he took that shot at us the other day," Joe added. "Remember, he was holding a rifle with a twenty-two barrel on it in that photo you saw."

"Rankin lives outside of Moody," Frank told his brother, "in a big house that hangs out over a cliff."

"You sure found out a lot in a few hours," Joe remarked.

Frank shrugged. "People in Alaska are real friendly. They like to talk."

Frank stood up. "You can catch a bus to Moody," he said. "Let's meet for supper at that pizza parlor at Lynx Creek Campground at six."

"It's a date," Joe said.

Joe went to the front desk to find out where he could catch the bus. The lodge looked deserted. Sandy was watching a small television behind the desk. Before Joe could ask her about Rankin, someone tapped him on the shoulder.

Joe turned to see Alex Loggins.

"What are you doing, Joe?" Alex asked.

Joe smiled. "Hey, it's good to see you. I'm trying to catch a bus to Moody."

"I've got a car," Alex said, "and I'm not doing anything this afternoon. I can give you a ride."

"If it's no trouble," Joe said.

Alex shook his head, then the two of them left the lodge. "What have you and Frank been doing?" Alex asked as they walked toward his car.

Joe decided to be vague. "We've done some traveling. We went to Fairbanks yesterday. Did you and Barbara see the salmon run?"

"It was awesome," Alex said. "Barbara did get a flight home on another airline, and I rented this car and drove back here. Today I took a helicopter ride around Denali."

"The whole park?" Joe asked.

"No, the whole *mountain*," Alex said.

"You mean Mount McKinley?" Joe responded. Then he remembered that Denali was the original native American name for the mountain. "Denali means 'high one,' right?"

Alex nodded. "It's the highest mountain in North America. Some people call it 'the Weathermaker' because the mountain creates storms when warm air hits it in the summer. The windchill factor at the top can drop to one hundred below in the summer."

Alex stopped at an orange compact car and unlocked it.

"Mount McKinley has the highest uplift of any mountain in the world," Alex added as they got in the car. "If you could take a tape measure and start at the bottom, measuring from base to peak, then McKinley would be about six thousand feet taller than Mount Everest."

Joe smiled. "I'm impressed, Alex. I bet my know-it-all brother doesn't even know that."

There were a lot of things Frank didn't know, and he was hoping a visit to Paul's cabin would reduce the number of unanswered questions.

The cabin was three miles from the park entrance. Frank drove over the one-lane gravel road that wound up the mountain. He was glad the rental agent pressed him to get a truck with four-wheel drive, because *road* was a very generous term for the rutted, rocky path. Frank glanced down at the trickle of a creek below and remembered how he and Joe had barely escaped crashing into that creek when someone took a shot at Paul's truck.

Frank parked around the back of Paul's cabin. It seemed that no one was home, which didn't surprise Frank because he doubted that a wanted man would hide out in his own house. Frank got out of his truck and headed straight for the front door. His boots shuffled over the gravel drive and made a hollow sound as he stepped up on the wooden porch.

As Frank reached for the front door handle,

he heard a strange sound, like that of someone plucking a flat guitar string. He started to turn. Out of the corner of his eye, he spotted a blurry shape hurtling through the air. The sharp steel tip of the arrow came into focus just before it was about to nail Frank right between the eyes!

Chapter

12

FRANK DOVE out of the path of the arrow as it whistled past and buried itself in the front door of the cabin with a solid *thunk*.

Frank didn't stop to admire the arrow's craftsmanship. He scrambled to his feet and leapt off the side of the porch into the bushes. Huddling down as low as he could, he peered out through the branches. He couldn't see anything, but he heard footsteps crunching on the gravel driveway.

Frank's only chance was to make a break for the woods. He took a deep breath and burst out of the bushes—and found himself staring into the sights of a loaded crossbow!

"Frank?" a familiar voice called out.

"Paul?" Frank responded, not sure if he should be relieved.

The man lowered the crossbow, leaving Frank with a clear view of Paul Garcia's haggard face.

"Sorry about that," Paul said. "I didn't realize it was you. It looked like somebody was trying to break into the cabin. It may seem like I over-reacted, but I honestly was aiming off to the side of you. I jiggled at the last second and the arrow was going to land dead between your eyes. I'm really sorry."

Frank nodded as he eyed the feathered shaft sticking out of the front door. "I didn't expect to find you here. Actually, I'm surprised the state troopers haven't staked out your place."

"They're watching it," Paul said. "One of their patrols drove by about an hour ago. That's why I was outside the cabin."

"Would you have shot at a trooper if he tried to go in the cabin?" Frank asked.

"No," Paul answered, "but I felt I had to try to stop a stranger. I've had a couple of break-ins over the past year."

Paul glanced around nervously. Frank could tell he was wary of being caught. Paul nodded toward the cabin. "Come on, let's get inside."

They went through the front door and sat down at Paul's kitchen table. "I figure as long as I don't turn on any lights and stay away from the windows, I'll be all right," Paul said, pulling up a chair. "Now, tell me what you're doing here."

"I was looking for—" Frank stopped himself.

"Paul, I have a few questions first. Why did you take off after the helicopter crash?"

"I didn't have any choice," Paul said. "After the crash, I searched for you guys. I landed about a half mile south of the chopper, down in a ravine. I got sidetracked by a grizzly in a bad mood and had to make a wide detour."

Paul got up and opened the refrigerator.

"I think Joe and I met the same bear," Frank said.

Paul handed Frank a cola. "Anyway," Paul continued, "I headed over to the chopper as soon as I could and saw you guys pulling the pilot out. Then I heard Dodge talking about me, like I had caused the crash!"

Paul gulped his soft drink. "That made me nervous. I was afraid those smoke jumpers might decide to play judge, jury, and executioner. When they hauled out the packs from the wreck, I grabbed one and took off. I knew that smoke jumpers carry food and extra clothes in their packs, and I wasn't sure how long I was going to have to be out in the woods."

Frank nodded. Paul might not have reacted the way Frank would have in the same situation, but Frank did understand why Paul ran away.

Frank sipped his cola. "How did you get back here?"

"I hiked over to the railroad," Paul replied. "It turned out to be only about five miles from the crash site. I spent the night in an old miner's shack near the track and then hopped a train this morning. I rode in the baggage car, jumped off near the park entrance, and then hiked home. I stopped at a store to buy a few things where nobody knows me."

"How long have you been here?" Frank asked.

"I got here about an hour ago."

"Why don't you turn yourself in?" Frank asked. "The state troopers won't hand you over to a lynch mob."

Paul shook his head. "Not until I find out who set me up. Did you and Joe talk to Rose?"

"Joe did," Frank replied. "Rose thinks Rankin is behind this."

Paul pushed his chair back and stood up. "And you guys believed her? Some nut case is out there burning down half the national park. Meanwhile, the state troopers are trying to make me take the rap for the whole thing!"

"Rose could be right, Paul," Frank said. "And she may not be as ruthless as you think. She told Joe she gave that hundred thousand dollars back."

Paul opened a cabinet door and cast a wary eye over his shoulder at Frank. "And you believed that, too. You guys are great. Thanks for your help."

"She may be right about Rankin," Frank persisted. "Joe and I think he might be the one who put that bullet hole in your truck tire."

Paul sat down at the table and opened a bag

of corn chips, pondering Frank's observation. Then he handed the bag of chips to Frank. "So what happens next?" Paul asked.

Frank reached into the bag and brought out a handful of chips. "Joe's out at Rankin's place right now. Let's wait and see if he comes up with anything."

Paul snorted. "Like a signed confession? Listen—do you guys really know what you're doing?"

Frank nodded. "We've done this before, Paul."

"I hope so," Paul replied, "because Rankin's not a nice guy. From what I've heard, he'll do anything to get what he wants."

"Do you think he'd sabotage a helicopter full of people?"

"Do you think Rankin is responsible for the crash?" Paul asked.

"Rankin was nosing around the helicopter just before we took off," Frank said. "The pilot went after him, and they had a little scene. We may not be able to prove that Rankin monkeyed with the fuel line, but he had the opportunity."

"So, are the troopers looking for him, too?" Paul asked.

Frank shook his head. "No. We have nothing on him. That's why Joe went out to his house, to see if he could find anything on Rankin."

Frank handed the chips back to Paul. "If you're not going to turn yourself in, you'd better stay out of sight. How do we get in touch with you?"

"I'll be around," Paul said, putting the chips in the cabinet. "It's probably better if you don't know where I am."

Frank went out the back door and walked around to his rented truck in the driveway. Frank climbed into the cab, started the engine, and backed down the long gravel drive. When he reached the road, he stopped and looked both ways, just as he would on a busy street in Bayport. He knew it was pretty silly in the middle of nowhere, but it was force of habit.

When he glanced off to the left, Frank spotted another truck parked on the side of the road. He was fairly sure state troopers didn't drive cherry red pickups. The truck might belong to somebody who lived nearby, but Frank didn't recall passing any on the way to Paul's cabin.

Suddenly the truck roared to life. The tires spun wildly, kicking up gravel and dirt. Then the truck shot straight at Frank.

Frank tried to slam the truck into gear, but he was too slow.

The mysterious cherry red pickup raced closer, so close now that it filled the passenger side window.

The truck kept coming. In a last ditch attempt to escape, Frank slapped the shoulder harness release with one hand and hit the door handle with the other. It was too late.

The impact from the collision hurled Frank across the cab. His shoulder slammed into a twisted, dented metal panel. A bolt of pain shot down his arm. Frank struggled back across the seat, pushed open the door, and tumbled out onto the ground. He crawled a few feet and then tried to stand up. He felt a little woozy, but thought he could do it.

Suddenly a meaty pair of hands was there helping him up. Then another rough hand clamped something over Frank's mouth. Frank tried to scream. The sickly sweet odor of chloroform filled his nose and mouth, and the world went black.

Chapter

13

ALEX SLOWED DOWN as they came up behind a
tanker truck driving north on Highway 3. "I
heard that Paul was arrested for starting those
forest fires. Can you believe that?"

Joe sighed, then launched into a short version
of everything that had happened to him and
Frank since they had seen Alex.

"I don't believe it!" Alex said. "We were with
Paul the whole time! How could he have started
a fire on that hike?"

"He could have set an explosive the day before, using a timer to make it go off," Joe explained. "Or at least that's a possibility we heard
from this Homer Dodge."

Alex speeded up as the tanker truck turned off

the road. "Why would Paul do that? Do you think he's guilty?"

Joe waited before answering a question that had been nagging him for two days. Then he shook his head. "No. But it doesn't help Paul's case that he ran away after the helicopter crashed."

They drove on in silence for a few more minutes until they reached a dirt road. Three miles down it Joe pointed to a split-level house on the side of a mountain, about two hundred yards away, and told Alex to stop.

"Who lives out here?" Alex asked.

"The king of disaster shirts, Jeff Rankin," Joe said. "The guy makes shirts that say things like 'I survived the Denali forest fires.' "

"Why are you going to see him?"

Joe hesitated, not wanting to reveal too much of what he was doing. "I've heard he's a pretty successful guy," Joe said. "So I came out here to learn some of his secrets."

The way Alex gazed at him, Joe could tell he was suspicious. Joe opened the door, started to get out, then turned to Alex. "Say, have you been to that pizza parlor in Lynx Creek yet?"

Alex nodded. "The reindeer sausage pizza is great. They have a good jukebox, too. A lot of people who work in the park and at the hotels go there after work."

"Do you have any plans for supper?" Joe

asked. "Why don't you meet Frank and me there about six?"

"Great!" Alex said. He looked at Rankin's house in the distance. "Is somebody here going to give you a ride back?"

Joe let out a low laugh. "I doubt it," he said. "I'll get back somehow, though. I'll meet you at Lynx Creek for supper. Thanks for the ride."

Joe shut the door and began hiking up the mountain toward Rankin's house.

Rankin's home was not a typical Alaskan wilderness house. Though it was made of timber and stone, it easily dwarfed any house Joe had seen around the park.

Rankin paid for this place running a lodge and selling T-shirts? Joe wondered. A four-car garage took up one end of the house. The building's right side hung out over the mountain, suspended by steel beams. It looked more like a country club than a home, Joe decided, catching glimpses of it as he climbed up the rocky hill.

Just then, Joe heard gunshots. He scrambled over a jumble of boulders and ran up the gravel driveway in front of the house. The gunfire was coming from the basement.

Joe took off for the left side of the house, sliding down a dirt and gravel embankment toward the basement windows. Another shot rang out, then another and another. Joe noted that whoever was doing the shooting wasn't worried about running out of ammunition.

He cupped his hands over one of the windows and peered into the darkness. He couldn't see anything. He tried to open the window. It wouldn't budge. He tried another window about ten feet away. It was locked, too.

The gunfire pounded out a steady beat.

His pulse quickening, Joe tried the last window on the end. He got lucky. The window squeaked open a crack.

The gunshots were louder now, clearly coming from somewhere in the basement.

Joe raised the window far enough to squeeze in. He climbed over the sill and dropped down on something that made a hollow, metallic *thunk.*

When Joe's eyes adjusted to the gloom, he realized that he had landed on a washing machine in a room about the size of a walk-in closet. The gunshots boomed and echoed through the basement. Joe winced and covered one of his ears to block out some of the noise as he got down off the washing machine.

There was a dryer next to the washer, and two doors enclosing them. Joe pulled one of the doors open to find a closet full of detergent and cleaning utensils. Light seeped through the bottom of the other door. Joe grabbed the knob and cracked the door just enough to peek out.

Rankin, the man Joe had seen arguing with Al Brunner before the helicopter crash, stood with his back to Joe, about fifteen feet from the laundry room. He was wearing headphones and shooting a pistol in what was an indoor firing range. The firing range was huge, with cinder block walls that ran the length of the house. Part of it was still used as a regular basement storage area, Joe realized. A bicycle and a dirt bike were parked in the shadows behind a stairway. In another corner, a computer sat on a table.

Rankin himself was about as tall as Joe but at least thirty pounds heavier—and those thirty pounds all muscle, Joe thought, noticing the ripples in Rankin's red T-shirt. He wore white jeans and fancy cowboy boots that Joe guessed were made from an exotic animal hide. As the man calmly squeezed off shot after shot, Joe cracked the door a little wider to see what Rankin was shooting at. A white outline of a man was his target. A photograph had been pinned over the head.

The face was very familiar. Moving closer, Joe realized that it was a photo of Paul Garcia!

Quickly Joe ducked back into the laundry room, his heart pounding with fear. If Jeff Rankin practiced shooting at a photograph of Paul, what was he willing to do to the trek leader in real life?

Just then, Joe noticed several boxes of bullets stacked on an ironing board to his right. Remembering the .22 bullet in Paul's truck tire, he spun around to take a closer look at the boxes—and accidentally bumped the ironing board, sending the board and the bullets crashing to the floor.

Rankin stopped shooting and raised his head—

phones. He turned around and peered back at the laundry room door. Joe shrank back into the darkness, out of the line of the thin shaft of light that pierced the laundry room. He couldn't see what Rankin was doing, and he waited tensely for the door to fly open. After about thirty seconds, the gunfire resumed.

Joe tried not to think about what would have happened if Rankin had stormed into the laundry room with a loaded pistol and discovered Joe spying on him. Joe waited another half minute, then crawled back to the door for another look at the boxes of ammunition on the ironing board.

He wasn't surprised to find that Rankin was shooting .22-caliber bullets.

A moment later Joe heard what sounded like a car or truck pulling up in the driveway. Rankin must have had a silent signal to tell when a car pulled up because he took off his headphones and went up the basement stairway.

Joe waited for Rankin to go through the door at the top of the stairs, then slipped out of the laundry room. He needed more evidence than a box of .22-caliber shells. He padded across the basement floor to the stairs, paused for a second, then tiptoed up to the door at the top. He pressed his ear against it and listened.

The only sound Joe heard was the wind brushing tree branches against the windows at the back of the house. Joe took a deep breath, opened the door, and carefully edged around the corner.

He tiptoed ten feet to another door, opened it slightly, and looked into a huge split-level den that seemed to run at least half the length of the house. He moved quietly through the room, past two blue leather couches and a gun case, then headed for a hall on the right. It led to the front door, which was wide open. Joe saw a living room to the right, stepped inside, and peeked through the drapes.

Two men were taking something out of the cargo bed of a pickup truck in the driveway. It took Joe a few seconds to realize that the men were hauling a body out of the truck. As the men dragged the limp form toward the house, the person's head lolled to one side.

Joe sucked in his breath. That was his brother they were carrying! It was impossible to tell whether Frank was alive or dead. Rage exploded in Joe's head. If these men had hurt Frank, Joe would make them pay.

Without warning something else exploded in Joe's head. A jagged edge of pain clouded all his thoughts, and darkness swept over him. Joe struggled to fight off the smothering blackness, but his body betrayed him, and he collapsed in a heap.

His mind held on for a few more seconds, screaming useless commands to his unresponsive arms and legs. He had to help Frank! But the darkness had engulfed him.

Chapter

14

JOE OPENED HIS EYES. There was nothing to see but darkness. Something was cutting into his wrists, and something hard pressed against his back. It took him a few seconds to realize he was sitting down and tied to a post.

He wasn't alone. He could feel somebody behind him, probably bound to the far side of the post.

Joe tried to move his hands. They were bound tightly behind his back. He took a deep breath and started to adjust to his surroundings. A line of light filtered underneath a door. Joe knew he had been here before, when the light was on. He was in Rankin's basement, underneath the stairway.

Then Joe remembered what he saw upstairs

before he was hit. Peeking through the drapes in Rankin's living room, Joe had seen two men drag Frank's limp body out of a red pickup truck.

Joe nudged the person behind him with his elbow. "Frank! Is that you?" he murmured.

Frank felt something prod him in the back. He tried to ignore it, hoping it would go away. He was so tired. He just wanted to sleep. Then he heard a voice that sounded as if it were coming from a great distance.

"Joe?" Frank mumbled. "What are you doing here?" Frank struggled through the fog in his brain and opened his eyes. "What am *I* doing here? Where are we?"

"Jeff Rankin's basement," Joe told him in a low voice. "Somebody sneaked up behind me and whacked me over the head. What happened to you?"

"I don't know," Frank said, his speech thick with sleep. "It's hard to think." He shifted his shoulder against the post and winced. The pain stirred his memory. "There was this red pickup truck. It smashed right into me—I mean into the truck I was driving. I tried to get away, but somebody grabbed me and drugged me."

"Rankin's men," Joe said. "I saw them. Are you okay?"

"I'm still groggy, and my shoulder hurts. I've probably got a big, ugly bruise from the crash, but I'll make it. How about you?"

"I've just got a sore head," Joe said.

Despite the situation, Frank had to chuckle. "That's nothing new. You've been a sore head most of your life."

"We've got to get out of here, Frank. Can you move your hands?"

"I'll try."

Joe felt fingers moving against his, and Frank grunted.

"Yeah, there you are," Frank said.

"Good," Joe answered. "See if you can loosen the ropes around my hands."

Frank struggled against the bonds. "No luck," he said. "You try me."

Joe gave it his best shot. "They're too tight." Joe leaned his aching head back against the post.

A moment later Frank murmured, "Why do you think they put us here, anyway?"

"I don't know," Joe answered. "Rankin has a firing range down here. He was doing some target practice before they brought you in. He was shooting a twenty-two."

Voices drifted down from the house above. Frank could hear Rankin berating a man named Scooter and another man named Buster.

"You got the wrong guy, you idiots!" Rankin yelled.

Joe nudged Frank. "Sounds like they're talking about you."

Rankin's tirade subsided, and Joe heard a rustling in the dark. It came from the direction of

115

the laundry room where Joe had hidden earlier. There was a faint click and a slight creak as the laundry room door swung open. A shadowy figure stood in the dim light that came from the window above the washing machine. The figure hovered in the doorway for a few seconds and then padded across the basement floor toward the Hardys.

A narrow flashlight beam pierced the gloom. The beam found Joe and moved up to his face, blinding him with white glare.

"You guys seem to like getting into trouble," a familiar voice said.

The flashlight beam moved off Joe and briefly lit the face of the intruder.

"Paul!" Joe whispered. "Where've you been?"

Paul knelt down beside them. "Shhh! It's a long story, Joe."

Joe waited for what seemed an eternity while Paul fumbled with the ropes tied around his wrists. Just as he sensed his arm was going numb, Joe felt a knot loosen. Finally he pulled his hands free.

"What are you doing here?" Frank asked as Paul untied him.

Paul loosened a knot on Frank's wrists. "I heard a car crash after you left my place," Paul whispered. "I ran up the road and saw two men getting out of a red pickup. The license plate said Hot Shirts—so I figured it must be Rankin's truck. I watched the guys put you in the truck, and then followed them here."

"In what?" Frank asked, pulling his hands free.

"The truck you rented," Paul answered. "What was left of it, anyway. It was pretty badly banged up, but it got me most of the way here. It died just before the turnoff to Rankin's house."

Frank stood up and flexed both hands to start his circulation. There was a noise overhead. Light streamed down the stairway.

Joe tapped Paul on the shoulder and pointed under the stairway. "Hide there," Joe whispered.

The Hardys hurried back to the post, sat down on the floor, and pretended to be tied up, gripping the post behind their backs.

Heavy boots tromped down the stairs. The basement light flicked on. A bald man with a fat paunch stood in the light.

He chuckled when he saw the Hardys. "Well, did you two have a nice nap?" he asked, sauntering toward them.

The bald man never saw what hit him. Paul lunged out from under the stairwell and clocked him over the back of the head with the flashlight. The man's eyes rolled up in his head. Then he crumpled to his knees and slumped over on the floor, his head falling in Joe's lap.

"Let's tie him up," Paul said, rolling the bald man over.

Joe grabbed the man under the armpits so he could lean him against the post. Paul tied him up, arms behind his back the way Joe and Frank had been bound.

"Okay, let's split," Paul said, heading for the laundry room.

Joe shut the laundry room door to muffle any sound of their escape. All three of them crawled up over the washing machine and out the window into the twilight. Joe glanced at his watch—almost eleven. He'd been out a long time.

Paul led them to the garage side of the house, then around to the big driveway. The red pickup that had rammed Frank's truck was parked in the middle of the drive.

Frank ran to the pickup and looked in the driver's side window. "No keys!" he said.

"Can you hot-wire it?" Paul asked.

Frank slid into the driver's seat. He fiddled with the steering column for a moment. Joe heard the engine turn over, then stop. It revved up again, then stopped again. Joe was getting more nervous by the second.

"Hurry up, Frank!" Joe whispered, drumming his fingers on the roof of the pickup. "Start it!"

While Frank leaned over the steering column and fumbled with the ignition wires, Joe nervously watched the house. A curtain drew back from a large picture window, and Rankin's angry face glared out at them. Rankin and Joe stared at each other for a second. Then the curtain fell back in place, and Rankin was gone.

"Rankin's spotted us!" Joe yelled. "Let's get out of here!"

Paul broke into a run around the back of the house. Joe followed, tearing through the stand of poplars at the side of the driveway.

Frank jumped out of the truck as Rankin and a big man with shoulder-length hair burst out of the house, both of them waving pistols in the air.

Joe glanced behind him as he turned the corner near the garage. He skidded to a halt when he saw Rankin and the other man bearing down on Frank.

"Keep going!" Frank yelled.

Frank tore across the driveway and around the corner of the house, only a few steps ahead of his pursuers. He slid down a hill behind the house, tangled vines tearing at his clothes.

Frank spotted Paul and Joe ahead of him, cutting across a ravine. Frank risked a peek over his shoulder and saw Rankin sliding down the hill.

Frank caught up with Joe and Paul on a trail leading up to a rocky peak.

"Did we lose them?" Paul asked.

"I don't think so," Frank said, puffing hard as he climbed over a rock. "I can't see them any more, but that may not mean anything. They could be coming at us from another direction."

Joe slid through a narrow opening between two

boulders. "Or maybe not. We're in good shape. Maybe we got away."

"Don't bet on it," Frank said, squeezing through the opening behind Joe.

The three of them bounded over the top of the peak and slid down a steep slope of gravel and dirt, maybe a hundred feet, to a ledge of rocks.

Below the ledge was a steep drop-off. At the bottom was a railroad track.

"What do we do now?" Joe asked.

"Somebody's going to break a leg if we jump," Frank said, huffing from the long run. "That must be a thirty- or forty-foot drop."

A long, high train whistle echoed through the hills.

An instant later a gunshot split off a chunk of rock near Frank's head. Rankin and the long-haired man came flying over the hill, shooting as they ran.

Joe ducked behind a boulder. Frank hit the ground, dragging Paul down with him. Then they scrambled for the cover of the big rock.

The train whistle wailed again, closer now.

"I can't see the train," Frank said, peering down the tracks.

"There!" Joe shouted. "Here it comes around the bend!"

Another gunshot zinged off the top of the boulder, spewing out a rain of rock chips. Frank knew that Rankin and his hired thug were closing in. They would probably split up and come around the boulder from both sides. Then there would be no escape.

The train roared underneath. Frank and Joe glanced at each other, and then at Paul. Joe shrugged and tried to smile. "Some vacation, huh?"

Frank didn't answer. Instead, he clutched his brother's hand, and together they leaped off the ledge.

Chapter

15

FRANK AND JOE crashed down onto the roof of the train as it trundled down the tracks. Joe stumbled and tottered on the edge. He couldn't get a firm footing. Just as he was about to tumble over the side, Frank clamped his brother's arm and pulled him back onto the roof.

Paul thudded down onto the car behind them. "Over here!" he yelled, scrambling for a ladder on the side of the train.

Frank and Joe crawled to the back of the train car. Joe had seen a lot of movies with guys sprinting across the tops of speeding trains, leaping from one car to the next. It looked great on the big screen. The real thing was a different matter. The train rocked and swayed as it bounced along the tracks. There was nothing to hold on to, and staring down at the ground whizzing past made Joe dizzy. He might not look like an action hero crawling along on his hands and knees, but he could live with that.

As the train rolled around a rocky bend, the Hardys followed Paul down the ladder and into a baggage car.

Inside, Frank slumped back against the wall of the car, exhausted. A dull throb pounded in his shoulder. He had pulled Joe back from the brink with the same arm that had gotten banged up in the crash.

Joe patted Paul on the shoulder. "Hey, thanks for getting us out of Rankin's place," Joe said. "We were in a tight spot back there."

"It's not the first tight spot we've been in on this trip," Frank said between heavy breaths. "Whenever we're around you, we seem to end up running from something."

"I've noticed that," Paul said, short of breath himself. He grinned. "And whenever I'm around you guys, something bad happens. If it's not a forest fire or someone shooting at us, then it's a helicopter crash. At the rate we're going, this train will probably derail."

"If Rankin and his sidekick don't catch us first," Joe agreed, sitting down next to Frank. "Do you think we lost them?"

"Would you make a jump like that if you didn't have to?" Frank asked.

"I guess not," Joe responded.

Frank raised a knee and rested his elbow on it. "Say, Paul, do you have any idea why Rankin's men would mistake me for you?"

Paul shook his head. "I've never seen them before," he said. "Maybe they've never seen me either. You and I are about the same height and have the same color hair. If all they had was a description, it would be easy to make that kind of mistake."

"Makes sense to me," Joe said, loosening the laces on his hiking boots. "I'll bet Rankin's the reason you're in this jam now, Paul. He was shooting a twenty-two down in his basement, with your photo as a target."

"Really?" Paul asked.

Joe nodded. "The guy's really got it in for you. Do you know why?"

"Maybe he thinks I was the one who undermined his bid for the park concession," Paul said, pulling a loose thread from a ragged hole in the knee of his jeans. "He could have heard a rumor that someone connected with Bull Moose Treks leaked his bid to SRO."

"But why would he go after you instead of Rose?" Frank asked.

"Well, I am the owner of Bull Moose Treks. Anyway, Rankin's a pretty macho guy. Maybe he assumed that because I was Rose's boyfriend I was the mastermind of the plan. Maybe he thought a woman wouldn't be as devious as a man."

"Rankin's pretty devious, that's for sure," Frank said. "He was nosing around the helicopter before we left the Eagle's Nest the other day."

Paul looked surprised. "He was?"

Frank nodded. "Just before we took off, Rankin was fooling around the chopper. The pilot caught him and tried to take a swing at him. Dodge broke it up and Rankin walked off."

Paul pulled another thread from the hole in his jeans. "Rankin has the know-how to sabotage a helicopter. He flew choppers in Vietnam, you know."

"What about the fires, Paul?" Joe asked. "Who do you think is behind them?"

"It's not me, and it's not Rose," Paul said. "Who can you think of who would profit from a forest fire?"

"Our friend, Mr. Hot Shirts," Joe said.

"Bingo," Paul said. "Rankin's made a small fortune selling those fire shirts—and he's mad about losing the park concession, too. My bet is that he started the fires to get revenge on SRO, while making up for his own losses at his lodge by selling shirts to fire fighters and tourists."

"And he sent his hired goons to take care of you," Frank said.

"Exactly," Paul replied. "But they got you by mistake."

"Then, Joe shows up in the wrong place at the wrong time," Frank continued. "Rankin couldn't call the sheriff's office to have Joe arrested for breaking and entering after Joe saw Rankin's men hauling me into his house."

Paul got up, walked over, and looked through the window on the door into the next car. "Uh-oh," he said. "Quick, get out on the ladder! Here comes the conductor! I can't risk being caught right now."

"You're not the only one," Joe responded. "We don't want that conductor to catch us without tickets."

Frank headed out the door at the other end of the baggage car.

The three of them climbed up the ladder and lay down flat on the roof. Joe stared at the observation car with its domed roof, three cars ahead. He hoped none of the passengers in the dome looked back and noticed three guys on top of the train.

"We'll wait until the conductor passes through to the next car," Paul said as the train rattled over a bridge. "Then we'll go back down."

Frank crawled back to the end of the car and peered over the edge, waiting for the conductor to pass between the cars.

Frank backed away from the edge when the door swung open. All he could see was the hat on the conductor's head. He waited for the man to go into the next car. The conductor paused, and Frank saw a wisp of smoke drifting away from the man's head. Terrific, Frank groaned inwardly. What a great time for a cigarette break.

Somebody should tell that guy that smoking is bad for his health.

A few minutes later the conductor finished his cigarette and went into the next car.

Frank climbed back down the ladder, followed by his brother and Paul. He grabbed the door-knob and tried to open the door. "Uh-oh," he murmured.

"What's wrong?" Joe asked.

"I can't open the door," Frank answered. "The conductor must have locked it!"

"We'll have to take our chances in one of the passenger cars," Paul said. "We may get lucky. Sometimes the evening train is pretty empty."

Paul led the way into the next car. Frank came through last and shut the door. He followed Joe and Paul up the aisle of a car full of compartments. The doors to the compartments were on the right, with windows on the left. Joe and Paul stopped to let a woman and a little boy pass.

The woman and boy entered one of the compartments. A moment later Paul tried the handle on another compartment. He slid the door open a few inches, then motioned Frank and Joe inside. They stepped in and locked the compartment door.

The three of them fell into the seats with relief. Frank and Joe stretched out on one seat. Paul had the other to himself. The two seats faced each other and were designed to slide together to make a bed. A bunk could be pulled down above one of the seats as well.

"By the way, Paul," Joe said. "Do you have any idea where we're going?"

"We're on the Midnight Sun, headed north to Fairbanks," Paul said. "The next stop is Nenana, about halfway to Fairbanks. We can get off there."

"Shouldn't we tell the police what happened?" Joe asked.

"I don't think that would be wise," Frank pointed out. "After all, you were breaking and entering, and Paul's still a wanted man."

"There's probably some kind of law against jumping onto a moving train, too," Joe grumbled.

Paul took a deep breath and gazed out the window. Then he threw up a hand, as if to wave off the Hardys' concerns. "Don't worry about me. Let's get off in Nenana, call the state troopers, and tell them everything. I can't stay on the run forever."

Just then the Hardys heard a commotion outside the compartment. Joe looked at his brother.

"Better check," Frank said. "It could be the conductor."

Joe slid the door open slowly, moving it just enough so he could stick his head out. A moment later he pulled his head back in. Joe tried to slide the door shut, but something caught in it. As he struggled to close the jammed door, Joe twisted his head and yelled, "It's not the conductor!"

Frank saw a hand come around the edge of the door from the outside.

"Hey, what's go—"

The question died on Frank's lips as Joe was shoved back against the seat where Paul was sitting.

The man who had pulled the door open stepped into the compartment. Another, larger man followed him inside. They were both holding pistols.

One of the men was wearing a red T-shirt. The other one had long black hair.

"Let me guess. I'll bet you guys didn't buy a ticket," Rankin said with a cold sneer.

Chapter

16

"SO," RANKIN SAID, "now we've caught all three of our housebreakers, Buster."

"And one arsonist," Buster added. Frank noticed a fresh scratch on the side of Buster's face, no doubt from the chase through the forest.

"Who knows?" Buster added, looking at Paul. "We might even get a reward for finding Mr. Bull Moose."

"I didn't break into your house," Frank said stiffly.

Rankin leaned back against the compartment door. "That's not the way I remember it. What I remember is that you and you and you"—pointing his gun at each of the Hardys and at Paul—"sneaked in through my basement window, and then—"

Suddenly the compartment went pitch-black. The train was passing through a tunnel.

"Nobody move!" Rankin ordered.

In the dark Joe lunged at Rankin and threw a body block at him, slamming Rankin's head against the door. Instantly the man went limp and slid down the door.

In the roaring echo of the tunnel, Frank's right arm shot out and slammed Buster's gun hand against the back of the seat. Frank's right hand pistoned upward in an open-hand karate blow aimed at Buster's jaw. The hard heel of Frank's palm caught the thug's throat instead. Buster collapsed, gasping for air.

Joe shoved Rankin out of the doorway and pulled at the door handle. "Let's get out of here!" he yelled as the train roared through the darkness.

Joe got a foot out the door and felt someone bump him in the back. "Okay!" Frank shouted. "Move!"

Frank heard footsteps behind him as he felt his way along the wall of the car. A gunshot rang out and a brief flash of light lit the corridor.

"Get down!" Paul yelled.

There was a shrill blast from the train whistle, and light flooded into the car as the train burst out of the tunnel.

Joe jumped up and ran for the rear door, about twenty feet away. He shot a quick glance behind him at Frank and Paul.

The three of them crowded together at the door as Joe fumbled with the handle. Another gunshot boomed through the corridor. Frank heard a scream from one of the compartments, but no one dared open a door. Joe glanced up to see that the bullet had cracked open the window of the car door about two inches above Joe's head.

"Don't move!" a voice yelled. Frank turned and saw Rankin lying on the floor, only half of his body in the aisle. The man had his gun leveled at the three of them.

Just then Joe worked the handle free, shoved the door open, and bolted out of the car. Frank and Paul raced behind him toward the door of the next car.

"No!" Frank called out. "It's locked!"

Joe turned and saw Frank scrambling over the safety railing. "Up the ladder!" Frank yelled.

Frank clambered up the ladder. The cool night breeze blew through his hair as the train whipped deeper into the Alaska interior. In the dusky light all Frank could make out were tall pines and dark mountains.

I can't believe this, Frank thought as Joe climbed up behind him. Hiding on the roof of a train going eighty miles an hour!

Joe fought off the fatigue that was starting to gnaw at him. The wind made it hard for him to keep a solid grip, but Joe held fast to the ladder and made his way slowly up.

On the roof, Frank and Joe pulled Paul up. Paul pointed toward the front of the train. "Let's find the conductor," he yelled.

As much as Joe hated the idea, he knew he was going to have to get up and run. There was no time to crawl. Rankin might be right behind them.

So Joe did what he knew how to do best—he stopped thinking. He leaped up, sprinted the length of the car, and jumped across the gap to the next car. He glanced behind him to make sure Frank and Paul were with him.

Halfway across the next car, the train went around a sharp curve. The unexpected turn to the left threw all three of them down and sliding across the metal roof to the edge.

Paul stopped himself by reaching down and grabbing the rail above the window. Frank actually thought he was going to fly off and smash into one of the boulders lining the track, but he pushed his hands flat and stopped himself at the rounded edge of the roof.

Joe went tumbling onto his side, and before he could get a grip on anything, his legs slipped over the edge.

"Hey!" Joe screamed.

"Hold on, Joe!" Frank hollered.

Joe clawed desperately at the roof, but his fingers just slid on the cold steel. As his legs sailed out into the air and he fell, Joe grasped the thin rail above the window, clinging to it with his fingertips.

Joe tried to pull himself back onto the train, pain shooting through his arms. The gale-force wind created by the speed of the train ripped at Joe, threatening to tear him loose.

Joe concentrated only on not letting go. Then he tried again to pull himself up.

It was no use. He was going to fall!

"Joe!"

In the twilight Joe could just make out his brother's face peering down at him from over the roof of the train, where he was lying down.

"Frank!" he cried. "I can't hold on any longer!"

"I've got you!" Frank shouted urgently. "I won't let go!"

At that moment Joe felt Frank grip his wrists.

"Paul!" Frank called out. "Grab my legs!"

Joe held his breath, trying not to think about what would happen if Frank's hand slipped.

"You have to help me," Frank told his brother in a steady voice. "Try to get some leverage with your feet."

Joe worked hard to wedge his feet against the side of the train. He couldn't get any traction until his shoes found a rubber lining along a window. Joe pushed with his feet as Frank hoisted him up.

Frank dragged Joe halfway onto the roof, and

Joe used his legs to push himself the rest of the way.

"That was—a close one," Joe panted.

"Garcia!" a voice bellowed.

It was Rankin. Frank realized that he had gone through the train and come out in front of them. Rankin was walking along the roof toward them, his gun trained on the trio.

Rankin stopped when he was about twenty feet in front of them. "Garcia!" he yelled. "You cost me a fortune!"

"How did I do that?" Paul yelled back.

"You know how! You and your girlfriend ratted to SRO about my bid!"

"Is that why you shot at Paul's truck?" Frank yelled. "Is that why you sabotaged the helicopter? All because you lost a business deal?"

Frank nudged Joe. Coming up, less than a quarter of a mile away, was a tunnel. Rankin couldn't see it; he was facing the rear of the train.

"You've got it all wrong, Jeff!" Paul yelled, with the tunnel only a hundred yards away. "I didn't have anything to do with that!"

Rankin sneered and nodded. "Sure you didn't!" he hollered.

The tunnel loomed up behind Rankin. "Look out!" Frank yelled at the top of his lungs. "Rankin! Duck!"

Rankin laughed. "Nice try. You must think I'm—"

Frank pulled Joe down flat against the roof of

the train. A second later they roared into darkness, the train's piercing whistle ringing in their ears.

His heart thudding in his chest, Frank took several deep breaths to calm himself. Too close, he thought. Everything on this trip has been too close.

As the train came out of the tunnel, Frank drew in a lungful of fresh evening air. It took at least a minute before the shock subsided and his muscles allowed him to raise up and look around.

"Where's Rankin?" Frank asked.

Paul lifted his head off the roof and turned to Frank. "He's gone."

Frank waited for Joe and Paul to go down the ladder. "Let's go find that conductor," Frank said as Paul hopped in front of the dining car.

Paul took a big breath, then exhaled. "Okay."

As it turned out, the conductor found them. He was coming through the dining car as the three of them walked in.

The conductor, a heavyset older man, glared at Frank, who came through the door first.

"Who are you?" he asked harshly.

"We jumped the train back around Moody," Frank said. "Two men with guns were chasing us. One of them's still on the train."

The conductor's eyes narrowed. "Where are these fellas you claim are chasing you?"

"One of them's about a mile behind us now, on the tracks," Joe answered. "He had an accident."

The conductor raised his eyebrows. "And the other one?"

Frank nodded past the conductor. "About three cars back, in a compartment," Frank said. "I think his name is Buster. When we went through the tun—"

"Take me to him," the conductor said brusquely.

In the compartment, they found Buster lying facedown. A red spot oozed below his left shoulder blade.

Frank knelt beside him and felt his neck for a pulse. After a few seconds Frank looked up at the others with a stunned expression. "He's dead. Rankin must have shot him by mistake in the dark."

The sky was a bright robin's-egg blue the next morning when Joe and Frank arrived at Fort Wainwright in Fairbanks. There were puffy clouds in the east, made golden by the sunlight.

They found Homer Dodge in the lounge on the first floor of the smoke jumpers dorm, reading the newspaper and drinking his morning coffee. Dodge's keen eyes fixed on the brothers as they came through the door.

"Well, this is a surprise," Dodge said. "Have a seat. What brings you boys here?"

"The train," Frank said, pulling back a chair. "With Jeff Rankin and one of his flunkies on it. They're both dead."

"Dead?" Dodge asked.

Frank told Dodge how Rankin and Buster had chased them and what happened on the train. Once the conductor had learned what had happened, he radioed the state troopers from the train, and they told him to keep Paul and the Hardys on board until Fairbanks. Two troopers met the Midnight Sun at the Fairbanks station.

After a long interrogation, Frank and Joe were released, and they checked into a motel in Fairbanks. Paul remained in custody, still under arrest for arson.

"Paul was framed," Frank told Dodge.

"Rankin was the one who took the shots at us, and he was the one who sabotaged the chopper," Joe added. "We think he set the fires to frame Paul, to get back at him for losing the park concession. Paul had nothing to do with his losing the bid, but Rankin didn't know that."

"Really?" Dodge said. "That's incredible." He stared at his newspaper for a moment, then pushed his chair back. "Of course, now that Rankin's dead, we'll never know if it's true, will we? Do you have any solid evidence that Rankin was setting fires?"

Homer was interrupted by a ringing telephone. "Excuse me a minute," he said, and went to answer it.

A minute later the smoke jumper came back to the table. "We've got another fire in Denali," he said, downing the rest of his coffee. "It looks like a big one, too."

On the way out of the lounge, the Hardys pelted Dodge with questions.

"Where is this fire?" Frank asked.

"The park service said it's in the Savage River area," Dodge replied. "It's about an hour from the park entrance by car."

"Do they have any idea how it got started?" Joe asked.

"Nope," Dodge said as he exited the room. "There hasn't been any rain or lightning in that area for months. That rain at Wonder Lake on Tuesday was just a localized thunderhead."

"This fire breaking out now should help Paul's case, don't you think?" Joe asked.

Dodge glanced quickly at Joe. "What makes you say that?"

"Because Paul was with us on the train when it started," Joe replied.

"So what?" Dodge asked. "It takes time, sometimes a day or two, for a fire to build up to where it can be sighted. An arsonist could rig up a device with a timer and make it go off hours later. Garcia could have started that fire while he was on the train with you."

"Rankin could have done the same thing," Frank countered.

They found Willis making phone calls at Dodge's desk.

"You heard about the fire?" Dodge asked him.

"I'm already calling the crew," Willis said, putting the phone down. "But I can't find the alternates, Homer. We're two men short because Carroll and Rocky are hurt."

"Get your two best rookies," Dodge told him.

"Hey, Homer," Joe said, "use me and Frank. We've already jumped, and we know how to dig a fire line."

"No way," Dodge said. "This is a real fire. You'd be crazy to jump into something like this."

"But, Homer," Joe started to say.

"No," Dodge snapped. "Absolutely not."

Joe tried another approach. "Can we at least ride on the plane?"

Dodge looked at Willis, who was punching numbers on the telephone. "We should have plenty of room," Willis said, not meeting Dodge's gaze. "We're only taking eight jumpers. These guys could drop the fire packs."

An hour and a half later the Hardys were sitting in the tail section of a DC-3, flying over Denali National Park. Wind rushed through the plane from the open door, where the smoke jumpers would leap into a world of flames.

Just as Frank and Joe got their first whiffs of smoke, the two rookie crew members began coughing, and one of them turned a sickly shade of green.

Dodge, looking out the door for the best jump site, shook his head. He said something to Willis, then walked back to where Frank and Joe were sitting with the fire packs.

"Okay, guys," Dodge yelled. "The rookies got smoke fever. We need you. Suit up."

Willis brought them yellow Nomex shirts and green pants, plus two hard hats. "You can use the rookies' packs," Willis told them.

Fifteen minutes later, as the plane made its third pass, Joe got a glimpse of the orange blanket rolling across the forest. A pall of smoke darkened the sky.

Joe hooked his static line—himself this time—and checked behind him to see that Frank did the same.

Seconds later Joe felt the tap on his left leg. He scanned the fire consuming the landscape, sucked in a deep breath, and stepped into thin air.

Chapter

17

FRANK LEAPED OUT and began counting. One thousand one—one thousand two—one thousand three—one thousand four . . .

Frank heard a rattle of fabric, and the chute grabbed him. He threw his head back to check the rigging. Everything seemed okay. Then he glanced down at the burning forest— things weren't so good down there, and he was drifting too close to the fire. Frank pulled on the toggle in his left hand, letting a jet of air escape from an opening in the back of the chute.

The chute swerved away from the fire as the ground came up fast. Frank clamped his feet together and rolled forward as he hit. His chute caught the wind and began to drag him toward the flames. Frank clawed at his harness release, but he couldn't get a grip on it.

The chute hit the fire and burst into flames.

Joe ran over to help Frank out of the harness, and they both scrambled away from the intense heat.

"That was a close one," Joe said.

"Yeah, I was about to get toasted," Frank said, wiping a film of sweat off his forehead.

It was a bad beginning, but Frank and Joe had no time to reflect. The roar of the fire sounded like a freight train. Trees and rocks were exploding from the heat, which Joe felt burning straight in his lungs.

"Over here! Hey!" a frantic voice screamed. "We're over here."

Joe spun around and saw a group of campers huddled around some boulders at the bottom of a hill. There were three men and two women. The fire was marching straight toward them.

Dodge came running out of the smoke. "Get them out of here!" he shouted to Joe. He pointed to a clearing about a half mile away. "Take them over there! If the wind changes, head for the creek."

The Hardys led the terrified campers to the clearing. When they got there, Frank spotted Dodge walking toward a sturdy rock cabin at the top of a ridge about two hundred yards away.

The cabin was framed by two tall pines but otherwise out of the timber.

"Let's take them there!" Frank hollered at Joe, who quickly nodded his agreement.

Frank led the way, and Joe brought up the rear, feeling the heat deep in his lungs every time he breathed. He knew the black creep of the fire was getting closer because it was harder to breathe.

Seconds after they were in the cabin, Dodge burst through the door. From the way he was staring at him, Frank thought the smoke jumper foreman was going to bore a hole in his forehead.

"I didn't tell you to bring them here!" Dodge yelled furiously.

"I'm sorry, Homer, I just thou—"

"Well, don't think! *I* do the thinking here." Dodge pointed behind the cabin. "Get these people down to the creek. Move it! That fire's headed this way!"

Frank decided it was better not to argue, and the Hardys took the campers down the ridge to the creek. Frank watched the blaze burn its way across the gulch, the wall of flame turning trees into torches.

A loud explosion thundered in the air.

"What was that?" a startled camper asked.

"Probably rocks," Frank said, remembering similar noises in the fire at Wonder Lake. "It's over a thousand degrees out there. Rocks and trees blow up from the heat."

144

Then Frank turned around and saw the cabin erupting in flames, the fire sweeping through the roof. Frank frowned in confusion. The forest fire hadn't reached the cabin yet.

"How are we going to get out of here?" asked another camper, a middle-aged man who looked as though he'd never been in the wilderness before.

"Until a rescue chopper comes, we'll just have to stay ahead of the fire," Frank replied. But he wasn't paying much attention to what he was saying. He was still staring at the cabin. The fire there soon burned itself out, starved for kindling.

"That was strange," Joe said to his brother. "It looked like the only thing flammable there was the roof."

Still watching the burned-out cabin, Frank saw someone walking through the rubble. He could tell it was a smoke jumper from the yellow shirt, but the fire fighter was too far away for Frank to tell who it was.

Frank told Joe to stay with the campers at the creek, then he ran up the hillside to the cabin. The rest of the crew was digging a fire line about fifty yards west of the creek.

Dodge was behind the cabin when Frank found him. The smoke jumper foreman had his back to Frank and didn't hear him over the noise of the forest fire. Frank was quite close by the time he realized that Dodge was digging a hole with the hoe end of his Pulaski. Beside the hole, Frank saw a short contraption about ten inches high, charred black by the fire.

The contraption was two dry cell batteries connected by wires to some sort of timer. Frank stared as Dodge, wearing gloves, reached for the object and began to bury it in the hole.

"Homer, what are you doing?"

Startled, Dodge whipped around. His eyes widened when he saw Frank, and he took a step forward as though trying to hide the hole. "Just doing mop-up work," he said to Frank. "We try to bury all debris and anything that's smoking."

"What is that thing?" Frank asked.

Dodge didn't answer.

Frank didn't wait long for a reply. "That looks like an incendiary device, Homer."

The foreman sighed and studied the object in the hole, then looked back at Frank. Without warning the smoke jumper grabbed his Pulaski and threw it tomahawk-style at Frank, who ducked as the tool flew by and clanked into a boulder.

"Hey!" Frank yelled, throwing his arms up as Dodge charged him, barreling into him and knocking him back into the rock.

Before Frank could recover, Dodge grabbed him around the neck, shoved his head against the boulder, and with his free hand reached out to grasp the Pulaski lying a few inches away.

"Wait!" Frank cried as Dodge raised the Pulaski. "Homer, we can talk about this!" It was no use. Dodge, his face red with fear and fury, was poised to deliver a fatal blow!

Frank had only an instant to wonder where all the other smoke jumpers were. What were the chances that one of them, in the midst of fighting the enormous fire, would happen to glance this way?

Suddenly Dodge was jerked backward, and Frank was free.

Joe hauled the hefty smoke jumper off his brother and wrestled him to the ground. Dodge struggled to get away, but Joe kept him pinned.

"Thanks, Joe." Getting to his feet, Frank brushed himself off. Then, still shaky, he stared down at Dodge. "That's an arson device you were going to bury, isn't it, Homer?" he asked, raising his voice to be heard above the fire.

No longer struggling, Dodge lay still and silent in the dirt, glaring at the Hardy brothers.

"You're the one who's been starting the fires, aren't you?" Frank pressed. "And you had that device timed to start another one today. But you didn't count on a natural fire spoiling your plans, did you?

"So the first thing you did when you landed was grab the device before anybody else stumbled across it, and you took it to the cabin to defuse it."

"But we showed up and almost caught you in the act," Joe said, catching on. "That's why you ordered us away from here. But after you got rid of us, there wasn't enough time left to stop the device from going off."

Dodge continued glaring at both brothers. Frank knew that, by not answering the questions, Dodge had given him his answer.

"I didn't hurt anybody!" Dodge suddenly shouted at them. "I just had to show people what I could do. I don't deserve to spend the rest of my life living off a lousy little pension!" The red-faced foreman thumped his chest. "I'm a legend! And I proved it."

Five hours later Frank was reaching for a slice of pizza at the Lynx Creek Campground Pizza Parlor. Here there were no flaming forests, terrified campers, or evil fire fighters. Here there was nothing but good pizza, good rock 'n' roll on the jukebox, and good friends, Alex, Paul, and Joe.

Paul had been released from jail in Fairbanks after the Hardys told the BLM investigators about Dodge. Willis and the other smoke jumpers had managed to dig a line that contained the fire before it reached the creek, and it was not long after that that the entire crew, along with the five stunned campers, had been lifted by helicopter out of harm's way.

"So Homer started the fires to have material for a book?" Frank asked Paul.

"Not just any book," Paul told Frank. "His autobiography—the story of the bravest smoke jumper who ever lived. Apparently, he had a

New York agent who told him the story would make a fortune, as long as it was dramatic enough. I guess Homer wanted to make sure it was dramatic, so he set extra fires in the most dangerous parts of the park. I hear he was negotiating a movie deal for the rights to his book."

Joe pulled off another slice of pizza. "Do you think it would make a good movie?"

"If they tell the whole story, sure," Paul said, taking a sip of soda. "The story of a man who wanted fame and fortune so much he was willing to burn thousands of Alaskan wilderness acres to get it. He sounds to me like the ultimate bad guy."

Frank wiped his mouth with a napkin. "I can see the blurb on the movie poster now. 'The daring exploits of a fire fighter who burned his way to glory.' It's twisted but definitely interesting."

"How did he set the fires?" Alex asked.

"The same way many arsonists do," Frank explained. "You rig up an explosive device. Homer made his with plastique connected to a battery and a timer, according to the state troopers. Then you set the timer and leave. During most of the fires, Dodge was able to sneak away from the other smoke jumpers long enough to bury the evidence."

"But then he started to worry that the BLM investigators were getting suspicious," Joe put in. "He decided someone else needed to take the rap before he was found out. Paul was a perfect candidate for a setup, since he'd already happened to be nearby when several of the fires started."

"All he had to do was check out one of Bull Moose's trek brochures and set the fire to go off at Wonder Lake while Paul was leading a hike through there," Frank finished.

Alex reached for another slice. "But what about the evidence in the back of Paul's truck?"

"Dodge stole a gasoline can with my fingerprints on it from my house a few weeks ago," Paul said. "And it was easy for him to add an arson device."

Frank nodded. "I remember you told me that there had been a couple of break-ins at your cabin."

"What about Willis?" Joe asked. "He certainly made a good suspect. He was reprimanded for—"

"Starting practice forest fires," Paul finished the sentence. "But it turns out Homer was responsible for those fires, too. Willis took the rap for him. Despite everything he's done, Homer Dodge still inspired that kind of loyalty."

"I guess I was wrong about Willis," Joe admitted. "That fouled static line on my parachute must have been an accident after all. But that didn't make it any less scary."

"Are we going to have to come back up here to testify later?" Frank asked.

"I doubt it," Paul said. "According to the state troopers, Homer has confessed to everything."

"What about Rankin's thug, the bald man?" Joe asked.

"Scooter?" Paul responded, grinning. "Scooter did a lot of talking to the troopers, too. He said that Rankin was the one who shot at my truck, but Scooter will still do time for assault and kidnapping."

"There's one thing I still don't understand," Joe said. "Did Rankin have anything to do with the fires?"

Paul shook his head. "Rankin just wanted to kill me. Homer and Rankin knew each other, but they weren't acting together. It was purely a coincidence that I figured into both their plans. If Rankin had known what Homer was up to, he might not have tried so hard to kill me—and he might still be alive."

Joe grabbed another slice, then pointed it at Paul. "Boy, Rankin sure was wrong about you, wasn't he?"

"That was my fault," said someone approaching the table.

Joe turned to see Rose. She was wearing jeans and a sweater and acted very subdued.

"Joe, I'm sorry about the way I treated you the other day," she said. "I understand why you thought what you did about me, considering what had already happened. You had every reason to be suspicious of me after finding that gun in my bag."

Joe put his pizza down. "Forget it," he said. "What are you doing here?"

Rose smiled. "This is a hangout for people who work in the park," she said. Then she turned to Paul, biting nervously on her lip before she spoke. "But I was actually hoping to see you, too, Paul. I hope you can forgive me for, uh, well, everything that's happened. Did Joe tell you that I gave—"

"Yeah," Paul said. He looked at Rose for a few seconds, then pulled a chair out for her. "Have a seat."

Rose sat down. "I've heard you three have been through a lot of misery this week because of me," she said uneasily.

Paul shrugged. "It wasn't your fault that Rankin had more than a few screws loose."

Rose gave Paul a nudge and smiled. "Thanks," she said. "Still, I have caused a lot of trouble this summer. I've also learned a lot about greed and what it makes people do."

"You're out of uniform," Joe observed. "Are you off duty?"

"For the next three months," Rose answered. "I'm on a leave of absence. I thought I'd take some time off and travel, to think about things. I'm taking the train to Anchorage tomorrow."

"Need a ride to the depot?" Paul asked.

Rose looked at him and smiled slowly. "Sure," she said shyly. "I'd love it."

"Where are you going after Anchorage?" Joe asked.

"I'm going to spend some time with my sister," Rose told him, "down in the lower forty-eight."

"We're headed that way, too," Joe said, wiping his hands on a napkin. "It's been a fun vacation, and I think we've gotten our money's worth."

Frank stretched. "I know I need some time to relax and cool down," he said. "This trip has been a scorcher."

Frank and Joe's next case:

The Hardys have come to the Hawaiian Islands to join in a scientific research project at the Mauna Kea Observatory. They have won the chance to witness a once-in-a-lifetime event—a total solar eclipse. But at the very instant day turns to night, the excitement suddenly turns deadly. The boys find the expedition leader . . . murdered!

Frank and Joe begin a research project of their own and make some shocking discoveries: The expedition has long been plagued by personal hatred, professional jealousy, and financial greed. They have plenty of theories but must come up with some hard facts. For evil lurks in the shadows, and more violence could erupt at any moment . . . in *Darkness Falls*, Case #89 in The Hardy Boys Casefiles™.

For orders other than by individual consumers, Archway Books grants a discount on the purchase of **10 or more** copies of single titles for special markets or premium use. For further details, please write to the Vice-President of Special Markets, Pocket Books, 1230 Avenue of the Americas, New York, NY 10020.

For information on how individual consumers can place orders, please write to Mail Order Department, Paramount Publishing, 200 Old Tappan Road, Old Tappan, NJ 07675.